Gretna, a slender girl with flowing spun-gold hair and a lovely wild-rose complexion, realized that the Marquis had been watching her. He was standing with his hands behind him, his dark head tilted back a little to see her, the expression on his face inscrutable, and his lips twisted in that strange, cynical smile.

She felt herself shiver a little and wondered what this ominous new life had in store for her.

Pyramid Books

by

BARBARA CARTLAND

DESIRE OF THE HEART
A HAZARD OF HEARTS
THE COIN OF LOVE
LOVE IN HIDING
THE ENCHANTING EVIL
THE UNPREDICTABLE BRIDE
THE SECRET HEART
A DUEL OF HEARTS
LOVE IS THE ENEMY
THE HIDDEN HEART
LOST ENCHANTMENT
LOVE HOLDS THE CARDS
LOST LOVE
LOVE ME FOREVER
LOVE IS CONTRABAND
THE INNOCENT HEIRESS
LOVE IS DANGEROUS
THE AUDACIOUS ADVENTURESS
THE ENCHANTED MOMENT
SWEET ADVENTURE
THE ROYAL PLEDGE
WINGS ON MY HEART
WE DANCED ALL NIGHT
THE COMPLACENT WIFE
A HALO FOR THE DEVIL
LOVE IS AN EAGLE
THE LITTLE PRETENDER
THE GOLDEN GONDOLA
STARS IN MY HEART
MESSENGER OF LOVE
THE SECRET FEAR
AN INNOCENT IN PARIS
METTERNICH, THE PASSIONATE DIPLOMAT
WHERE IS LOVE?
TOWARDS THE STARS
DESPERATE DEFIANCE
RAINBOW TO HEAVEN
DANCE ON MY HEART
THIS TIME IT'S LOVE
ESCAPE FROM PASSION
AN INNOCENT IN MAYFAIR
THE WINGS OF LOVE
THE ENCHANTED WALTZ
THE HIDDEN EVIL
ELIZABETHAN LOVER
THE UNKNOWN HEART
OPEN WINGS
AGAIN THIS RAPTURE
THE RELUCTANT BRIDE
THE PRETTY HORSE-BREAKERS
THE KISS OF THE DEVIL
A KISS OF SILK
NO HEART IS FREE
LOVE TO THE RESCUE
STOLEN HALO
SWEET PUNISHMENT
LIGHTS OF LOVE
BLUE HEATHER
THE IRRESISTIBLE BUCK
OUT OF REACH
THE SCANDALOUS LIFE OF KING CAROL
THE THIEF OF LOVE
WOMAN, THE ENIGMA
ARMOUR AGAINST LOVE
JOSEPHINE, EMPRESS OF FRANCE
THE PASSIONATE PILGRIM
THE BITTER WINDS OF LOVE
THE DREAM WITHIN
THE MAGIC OF HONEY
A HEART IS BROKEN
THEFT OF A HEART
ELIZABETH, EMPRESS OF AUSTRIA
AGAINST THE STREAM
LOVE AND LINDA
LOVE IN PITY
LOVE AT FORTY
THE ADVENTURER

LOVE IN HIDING

Barbara Cartland

PYRAMID BOOKS ▲ NEW YORK

LOVE IN HIDING

A PYRAMID BOOK

Pyramid edition published October 1969
Tenth printing, August 1977

Printed in the United States of America

Pyramid Books are published by Pyramid Publications (Harcourt Brace Jovanovich, Inc.). Its trademarks, consisting of the word "Pyramid" and the portrayal of a pyramid, are registered in the United States Patent Office.

PYRAMID PUBLICATIONS
(Harcourt Brace Jovanovich, Inc.)
757 Third Avenue, New York, N.Y. 10017

1

THE STAGE-COACH had made good time since it left the posting-inn at Hartley Wintney. The horses were fresh, and as if they were anxious to make up for the irritating delays which had made the coach nearly three hours late, they moved at a spanking pace along the narrow, twisting lanes which led towards Blackwater.

But if the horses were fresh, the coachman was the opposite. The ale at the inn had been strong and he had been kept awake the night before with a nagging tooth. He yawned loudly, making his companion on the box—a thin, nervous little man with spectacles—look up at him apprehensively.

He yawned again and did not seem to notice the sharp corner ahead until they were almost on top of it, and then as the horses, still travelling too fast, seemed to become aware of a bend in the road, a curricle, travelling at quite a formidable speed, came into view. There was a flash of yellow-and-black wheels, a glimpse of a pair of perfectly matched chestnuts, a Gentleman wearing a beaver hat at a jaunty angle holding the ribbons, and another equally smart seated beside him.

Then the thin man in spectacles let out a cry of sheer terror. The coachman tugged at the reins, but it was too late.

The horses swerved sharply, suddenly aware of the danger. Then, by a superb piece of driving, the curricle, scraping the wheel of the coach, got past. But after seeming for a moment to rock like a clumsy wooden ark, the coach crashed against the bank and partially overturned, the horses plunging and rearing.

For a moment there was pandemonium. A woman screamed, violent oaths were shouted—some in fear, some in anger—and then a voice, cold, contemptuous and authoritative, seemed to restore sanity.

"Get to your horses' heads, you fools!"

The coachman scrambled to his feet followed by the groom who appeared from the ditch with a bemused expression on his face as if he had been asleep before this happened.

The thin traveller in spectacles climbed down on to the road.

"Th . . . this is m . . . monstrous, m . . . monstrous!" he said in a quavering voice to the driver of the curricle.

"I agree with you, Sir," the Gentleman answered. "Your driver is either a knave or a lunatic to approach a corner at such a speed. But no good will be served at this stage by recriminations. I suggest you assist the inside passengers to extricate themselves."

The traveller, who was about to say a great deal more, obviously lost his nerve. He bit back the words that seemed to tremble on his lips and turned, as he was bid, towards the coach.

The horses were being held and now that the moment of panic was past it was obvious that things were not so desperate as they had seemed in the first moment of the accident.

The coach lay a little drunkenly against the raised bank and it appeared that the nearside wheel was damaged. Otherwise the disaster seemed slight.

It was then that through the lowered window a Vision appeared and a soft little voice asked a little breathlessly:

"What has happened?"

The face was entrancing. Small and heart-shaped, it possessed a tiny, tip-tilted nose, a full red mouth and two large blue eyes. These were all framed by a profusion of gold curls that had escaped from a chip straw bonnet which, in the confusion, had fallen on to her shoulders.

"Allow me, Madam."

Another voice spoke now and a young gentleman who had been the passenger in the curricle, gorgeously attired in skin-tight buckskin breeches and a dazzling blue satin coat, climbed down and, hurrying forward, swept his high-crowned hat from his head.

"Oh, wait a minute!" the Vision said as he put out a hand to open the door. "We are in a vast confusion."

She disappeared from the window; and then, as the young gentleman, pulling with all his strength, managed to open the door, it was to find himself assisting another lady to alight.

Fat, buxom, with a red face and brown eyes swimming with tears, she heaved herself with some difficulty down on to the roadway, exclaiming as she did so:

"Lawks amercy! I never did trust these darned coaches and I never shall."

The young gallant supported her arm, but it was obvious from his glances over her shoulder into the interior of the coach that he was more concerned to see the Vision again than in proffering his help from a humane point of view.

The Gentleman who had driven the curricle and ordered the coachman to the horses' heads, sat watching with the faintest smile on his lips, a quizzical look in his dark, hard eyes.

The Vision reappeared.

"Are you all right?" she asked anxiously, speaking not to the gallant waiting with outstretched hand to assist her to alight, but to the stout woman now standing in the roadway.

"Quite all right, thank you, dearie. Although I'm as sure as I'm standing here that every bone in my body is bruised or broken."

The Vision laughed and then, taking the hand that was proffered to her, seemed to float on to the ground as lightly as a piece of thistledown.

"Are you certain you are not hurt, Madam?" her assistant asked, holding her hand a little longer than was necessary.

"Oh, quite, I thank you," she replied. "But I am afraid the other traveller with us is badly bruised. We all seemed to fall on top of him."

She turned back and smiled at an elderly man who must have been a schoolmaster, who was descending with a little carpet bag in his hand.

" 'Tis lucky we are alive, that's what I say!" the stout woman ejaculated. "We were travelling too fast, and nobody's going to tell me that we weren't."

"You are undoubtedly correct, Madam," the Gentleman in the curricle agreed. "And I beg of you to say so when you reach London. Your coachman was entirely at fault."

"And how am I to be sure that you were not to blame as well, Sir?" the lady asked, obviously determined not to be browbeaten and have other people's opinions thrust upon her.

"We had best introduce ourselves," the young gallant who had assisted her from the coach said, with his eyes on the Vision. "I am Sir Harry Carrington, at your service,

Ladies, and this is the Marquis of Stade, one of the most noted whips in the country."

The stout lady dropped a curtsy.

"I'm sure, m'Lord, that no offence was meant."

"And your name?" the young gallant asked the Vision eagerly.

"My name is Gretna——" she began, only to be interrupted by the stout woman.

"My name is Merryweather, if it pleases your Lordship. Mrs. Merryweather of Brambridge Farm near Winchester, and this is my niece who is travelling to London with me. And now, if you gentlemen will excuse us, we had best find our way to the nearest village and wait there until the wheel of the coach is repaired."

"Oh, but you cannot do that," Sir Harry exclaimed. "We must find you somewhere more congenial to rest, must we not, Julien?"

He turned to the Marquis, an eager look on his face, and Lord Stade, still with that cynical twist of his lips, replied suavely:

"Indubitably. If the ladies will permit me to drive them to Stade Hall, which is only a few miles from here, I will instruct my own blacksmith to see to the repair of the wheel."

"That's very kind of your Lordship," Mrs. Merryweather said, "but my niece and I will manage well enough in the inn."

"Oh, but . . . why?" her niece asked. "I think we should accept such a kind invitation. It may be some hours before the coach is ready to proceed."

"That is very sensible," Sir Harry approved.

The Marquis waved his whip in the direction of the two other travellers who had been listening to this exchange of pleasantries.

"If you gentlemen care to walk half a mile down the road you will find a small hostelry. Tell the landlord I sent you and he will do his best for you."

"Thank you, m'Lord."

The elderly schoolmaster and the thin man in spectacles accepted the suggestion, although they looked a little enviously at the two ladies being helped up into the curricle.

It was hard to think that the two could be in any way related. Mrs. Merryweather, with her large, bulging figure and fat, red face, looked a typical farmer's wife; while the slender girl following her, with her lovely wild-rose complexion and spun-gold hair, seemed to belong to another world.

But there was no mistaking the poverty of her plain stuff gown or the severity of the untrimmed bonnet with its cheap ribbons which she now hastily pulled over her curls.

Perhaps she was going to London to seek a position as a housemaid, Sir Harry mused to himself. Or maybe she would find employment as a governess. Whatever it might be, it was a demned shame that anyone so pretty should have to earn her own living.

The curricle, which had obviously been built for speed, was not a particularly suitable vehicle for ladies. Mrs. Merryweather refused to climb up on the box beside his Lordship.

"I'll sit behind," she said, "and Gretna will sit beside me. You gentlemen are best in front where you were when you overturned us."

"Now, now, Mrs. Merryweather!" Sir Harry admonished. "You must not say that. It was your coachman who overturned you, not us."

"Well, that's as maybe," Mrs. Merryweather retorted. "Anyway, Sir, that's the way we'll sit."

Sir Harry was obliged to acquiesce. He had obviously had ideas of putting her on the box beside the Marquis and sitting with her niece at the back. But Mrs. Merryweather was too firm for him and he was forced to do as she wished, only turning round, endeavouring to see the pretty, heart-shaped face that was almost obscured from him by the ugly bonnet.

Gretna tried to say something to Mrs. Merryweather, but the latter put her fingers to her lips and she lapsed into silence, content to watch the countryside as they hurried back along the road down which they had just come. After perhaps a mile the curricle turned through some fine ornamental gates into a drive bordered with oak trees.

Sitting where she was, Gretna did not see Stade Hall until they had passed through a second pair of gates which led into the courtyard and swung round in front of the wide stone steps which led to the front door.

Then she gave a little gasp of surprise at the magnificence of it. There was no doubt about it at all, it was a very beautiful house set like a jewel in green parkland, with great trees shading a small herd of speckled deer.

There was a lake, shimmering golden in the evening sun, and smooth lawns which reached down to the edge of the lake.

She had, however, little time to look around her before a footman, with powdered hair and claret-and-gold livery, was assisting her to alight and she and Mrs. Merryweather were led by Sir Harry into a huge, porticoed hall.

"You will wish some refreshment, I am sure," he said eagerly. "Do you not agree, Julien? They must be very shaken by the accident."

"Wine and biscuits are to be served immediately in the Salon," the Marquis said to the butler in what seemed to Gretna to be an uncompromising, autocratic voice, as if he was not particularly pleased at the idea.

"And now, ladies," he added, "I am sure you would like my housekeeper to show you to a bedchamber where you can wash and tidy yourselves."

"We should be glad of that, m'Lord," Mrs. Merryweather answered. She curtsied and Gretna followed her example, and then they walked up the broad staircase to where, at the top, a housekeeper in rustling black satin stood waiting for them with folded hands.

She seemed to take in Mrs. Merryweather's status at a glance, and with a slight sniff, as if to wait on such a person was beneath her dignity, she led the way to a large bedroom.

"The chambermaids will bring you hot water and anything else you require," she said, and withdrew, leaving them alone.

Mrs. Merryweather looked around her.

"Lord love us, what a room!" she said. " 'Tis many years since I have seen the like. Those tapestries are worth a fortune if they are worth a penny."

"Mrs. Merryweather, why did you say I was your niece?" Gretna asked.

Mrs. Merryweather turned her brown eyes from the tapestries to look at the exquisite, heart-shaped face beside her.

" 'Twas the best thing to do, dearie," she answered. "And you're not to tell them your name, do you understand now?"

"Why not? They are not likely to know who I am."

"But they are. Your mother will not have been forgotten, even though Society has not seen her these eighteen years."

"But even if they do know, does it matter?" Gretna enquired.

"Indeed it does," Mrs. Merryweather answered. "Now, see here, Miss Gretna. I was in service thirty years ago, before I married my Tom. I never rose to anything grand, mark you—only fourth housemaid to Lady Lansdale—but I learnt what was right and what was not. And one thing I can tell you for certain sure: no young lady in your position should be gallivanting off to London alone on a stage-coach."

"But I am not alone and I am not gallivanting," Gretna smiled.

"I know that, dearie, I'm with you, but it was just a bit of luck that I could go at this moment to visit my poor sick sister at St. Albans, and you're going because you has to. At the same time, you cannot explain those sort of things to gentry. They wouldn't understand."

"But it cannot matter to them," Gretna argued.

"Now, listen, dearie! You don't know anything about life—living that quiet with your mother, hardly seeing a soul since she's been ill. You're grown up now, you're seventeen, but there's a lot for you to learn and the first lesson is don't trust no gentleman—not of the type of these two at any rate."

"Why, what is wrong with them?" Gretna asked wonderingly.

"Well, it seems to me that I've heard of the Marquis," Mrs. Merryweather answered, her brow wrinkling as if in the effort to remember. "And what I have heard ain't much to his credit either. And as for the other, Sir Harry whatever he calls himself, I know his type right enough. Out for a bit of fun whoever pays for it, and every pretty girl be fair game."

Gretna gave a little laugh of sheer amusement.

"Oh, Mrs. Merryweather, you are funny! I do not believe they are half as bad as you are painting them. They seem to me very kind, although I must admit the Marquis seemed rather frightening and was not over-anxious to offer us his hospitality. I think Sir Harry forced him into it."

She gave a little sigh.

"At any rate, 'tis only for a few hours. I cannot come to any harm in that time."

"Don't you be too sure," Mrs. Merryweather said darkly.

"I could tell you some tales. You can't trust these young sparks."

"Well, with you to protect me I shall be absolutely safe, as if I was sitting at home in my own little cottage," Gretna said soothingly. "But tell me what you know about Lord Stade."

Mrs. Merryweather was about to reply when the door opened and two chambermaids, wearing crisp mob caps, came hurrying in with jugs of hot water. They poured them into two basins standing on the marble washstand, added rosewater and laid ready two soft linen towels edged with lace.

"Thank you so much," Gretna said gratefully.

"Is there anything else you want, Miss?" one of the chambermaids asked. "There are clean brushes and combs on the dressing-table."

"That is all I require, thank you," Gretna replied.

She took off her bonnet and washed her face and hands, feeling fresher as the dust of the journey was removed by the scented water. The towel was deliciously soft and when she had dried her face she walked across to the dressing-table to comb her fair curls into some semblance of order.

"We never thought, when we set off this morning, that we should end up in a house like this, did we, Mrs. Merryweather?" she asked. "It's a real adventure!"

"The sort I, for one, don't appreciate," Mrs. Merryweather retorted. "I want to get you to London safe and sound and the sooner the better says I. This sort of thing ain't going to do us any good."

"Oh, Mrs. Merryweather! Do look on the bright side of things," Gretna begged. "I am sure neither Lord Stade nor Sir Harry means us any harm. Indeed, what harm could they do us? And this house is magnificent. I thought Mr. Smythe's house was fine, but this is infinitely finer. Did you see the marble pillars in the hall, the pictures on the walls and the carved newels on the staircase?"

"Let's hope that dratted coach is repaired quickly," Mrs. Merryweather said darkly. "Just our luck that one of the horses losing his shoe made us so late that half the passengers cried off. If there had been another half-dozen, as there should have been, his Lordship wouldn't have been so ready with his invitation."

"I do not comprehend why you are worrying," Gretna laughed. "I am looking forward to the glass of wine and the biscuits the Marquis promised us. Come along, let us go downstairs."

She opened the door and led the way while Mrs. Merryweather came panting behind her.

It was a lovely house, there was no doubt of that. If the hall was magnificent, the Salon into which the footman showed them was beautiful. Hung with delicate rose-pink brocade curtains, it had big crystal chandeliers which glittered from the sunshine coming in through the long windows, while the elegant inlaid furniture was a perfect background for china, ivories and other elegant *objets d'art.*

Sir Harry was standing by the fireplace and hurried forward eagerly at their appearance.

"Here you are!" he exclaimed. "I've been in the deuce of a pucker lest you should be the worse for the accident."

"We are in excellent health," Gretna laughed. "Mrs. Merryweather and I are only so mortified that we must put you to all this inconvenience."

She glanced as she spoke towards the Marquis who had not moved from his position near the fire. She had not realised how tall he was or how broad-shouldered. He was exceedingly handsome, but his face wore a disagreeable expression. She thought too that his cold eyes rested on her almost with an expression of disdain, and she found herself blushing.

"But it is no inconvenience—we like it above all things," Sir Harry was expostulating. "Do we not, Julien?"

He glanced towards the Marquis as if forcing him to answer his question, and almost reluctantly, it seemed to Gretna, the Marquis's lips moved.

"It is, of course, a pleasure."

Could any other man, she wondered, have made those last two words sound so sarcastic?

A footman offered Mrs. Merryweather a glass of Madeira and then brought one to Gretna. She took the glass, sipped it and then made an almost involuntary little grimace.

"You do not like it?"

It was the Marquis who asked the question and she glanced up at him a little apprehensively.

"No, indeed, it is very . . . pleasant," Gretna said hastily.

The Marquis turned to the footman.

"Take the lady's glass away and bring some tea immediately."

"Very good, m'Lord."

"Oh, but I would not . . . put you to so much trouble," Gretna faltered.

"It is no trouble," the Marquis said, and this time there was no sarcasm in his voice. "Wine is for those who like it. For those who have not acquired the taste it is quite unnecessary to force it upon them."

"Tea! I should never have thought of that," Sir Harry exclaimed. "But, of course, that is the beverage my sister prefers."

The Marquis looked at the clock on the mantelpiece.

"And that reminds me, Harriet will be waiting for you," he said. "The horses are at the door. Pray convey my apologies to your sister and say I shall hope to wait on her tomorrow."

"Stop me, Julien!" There was no mistaking the protest in Sir Harry's voice. "I'll be hanged if I leave now. Harriet can wait."

"On the contrary," the Marquis replied. "We contracted to be at Bridgewater Place by five o'clock. As it is, you will be nearly an hour late. There is no reason to incommode your sister any further."

" 'Pon my soul! Harriet's party is of little consequence to me. And what about you?"

The Marquis smiled.

"As I have already requested you, Harry, please convey my regrets. But, if you recall, I had always intended to dine here. I am not interested in formal parties such as will take place at your house this evening."

"I told Harriet she was betting on an outside chance," Sir Harry replied. "But she hoped that you might be persuaded."

"Your sister is always most kind," the Marquis informed him formally.

Still Sir Harry hesitated. Gretna could see that he was longing to make some excuse or put up some argument in favour of his staying. It was equally obvious that the Marquis intended him to go. The older man won.

"Rum sort of hospitality in Stade Hall!" Sir Harry complained. "All right, I'll go, but remember, Julien, I do so under protest."

He took Gretna's hand in his.

"Good-bye, Miss Gretna. I am determined that we shall

meet again. Will you tell me your address in London so that I may pay my respects?"

Gretna's eyes dropped before his.

"I am not . . . certain . . . where I shall be . . . staying," she stammered.

"Oh Lud! That means I must search the whole city until I find you," Sir Harry said despairingly. "Give me just a glimmer of where you might be or the name of some friend where I could enquire of you."

"Now, now, young man," Mrs. Merryweather interposed. "My niece has said she doesn't know where she will be staying. Best leave it at that—though I'm sure you mean well, Sir."

"I do indeed, Mrs. Merryweather!" Sir Harry assured her. "Well, perhaps you will be gracious enough to confide in Lord Stade before you leave. I shall be consumed with anxiety to hear that the accident has had no serious effect on you—as well as your niece."

"Get along with you, Sir, that's just an excuse and well you know it," chuckled Mrs. Merryweather. "Thank you for your help, though. You've been kind, I'll say that for you."

"That is a recommendation in itself," Sir Harry laughed as he turned towards the door.

"I'll never forgive you for this, Julien," he said. "I've a good mind to call you out for it. I shall detest every moment of Harriet's dinner-party and be in such a fit of the sullens that she'll be incensed with you too, when I tell her the reason for it."

He opened the door. Then he looked back at Gretna.

"*Au revoir,* Miss Gretna," he said softly. "I am convinced that we shall meet again very soon."

He departed, slamming the door behind him. The Marquis reached towards the bell.

"I will enquire how far your coach has progressed," he said. "There should be news by this time."

The door opened again to admit a footman with the tea that had been ordered for Gretna. It was served on a silver tray from a beautifully chased silver teapot and the cup from which she sipped it was of such thin china that it was almost transparent.

Gretna's eyes wandered round the room.

"Oh!" she exclaimed with a little lilt in her voice. "I see you have a Van Dyck, and what a beautiful one! Mamma always used to say that one could never mistake a Van

Dyck because of the hands. How beautifully that man's hands are painted."

The Marquis's eyebrows went up.

"He was one of my ancestors," he explained. "But I am surprised you should recognise the artist."

"Surprised?" Gretna questioned. Even as she spoke she realised that his surprise was due to the fact that he thought her to be Mrs. Merryweather's niece, and she felt the colour come into her face as, with difficulty, she stifled the retort that although she might be poor she had been well educated.

"He is arrogant and overbearing," she thought, and suddenly resented the fact that he had sent Sir Harry away when the younger man had wanted so much to stay. "I suppose everyone must obey his commands," she thought, and noticed the disdainful manner in which he took a note from the silver salver which had been brought to him by a footman.

He read the piece of paper through his quizzing glass and then laid it down again on the salver.

"I am afraid, ladies, I have bad news for you," he said. "My agent informs me that the coach cannot possibly be ready tonight. Only by working on it for at least another six hours will it be in sufficient repair to leave for London tomorrow morning."

"That is bad news, indeed!" Mrs. Merryweather ejaculated. "I said our luck was out from the very first thing this morning. Well, m'Lord, we must thank you for your hospitality and see what sort of accommodation we can get at the local inn. There is one, I think you said."

"Naturally you will stay here," the Marquis answered.

He turned to the footman as if there was no question of there being any argument in the matter.

"Tell the housekeeper to have two bedchambers prepared immediately, and send to the coach to collect these ladies' baggage."

"Very good, m'Lord."

The footman withdrew as Mrs. Merryweather, growing a little red in the face, expostulated:

"This is quite unnecessary, m'Lord."

The Marquis smiled, that same cynical, twisted smile which had, it seemed, very little humour in it.

"However reluctant you may be to accept my hospitality, Mrs. Merryweather, you cannot expect me to turn you out at this hour in the evening," he said. "Besides, I promise you that the village inn is very uncomfortable and not at all suitable for anyone with the countenance of your niece."

"Very well, m'Lord." Mrs. Merryweather was defeated and she knew it. "And we must thank you for being so accommodating in this matter."

"We must, indeed," Gretna said warmly. "And I must be truthful and say I am not sorry for what has happened. This house is so lovely and you have so many beautiful things, m'Lord. May I look at them?"

"I shall be delighted," the Marquis said. "But we dine at seven o'clock. Perhaps you ladies will wish to repair to your rooms. Your baggage will not be long in arriving."

"I'm sure, m'Lord," Mrs. Merryweather said a little hastily, "that you would wish us to dine upstairs. It must be an inconvenience to your Lordship to entertain us."

"If it were, Mrs. Merryweather, I should not hesitate to say so," the Marquis replied. His dark eyes met Mrs. Merryweather's troubled brown ones, and Gretna, watching them, fancied there was a faint glitter in the Marquis's as if he relished overthrowing the obstacles that were being put in front of him.

Gretna rose to her feet.

"Thank you very much for having us," she said, rather like a child who has been reciting something that she had been told to say.

The Marquis turned his eyes upon her.

"I hope that you will not be disappointed in Stade Hall," he said. "It will give me much pleasure to show you some of its treasures after we have dined."

Even as he spoke Gretna was aware that his words were directed more at Mrs. Merryweather than at herself. Once again she thought how autocratic he was. He could not bear opposition; he would fight it wherever he might encounter it and even if it came from someone so insignificant and unimportant, in his eyes, as fat Mrs. Merryweather.

As they went up the stairs side by side, Gretna slipped her arm into the older woman's as if in some wordless way she would thank her for trying to protect her. Even as she did so, she realised that Mrs. Merryweather's breath was coming unevenly and her cheeks, instead of being their usual rosy red, had become almost purple.

"What is the mattter?" Gretna asked anxiously.

" 'Tis a pain just here," Mrs. Merryweather said, putting

her hand below her breast. "It's fair cutting into me, dearie, I can tell you. Just like a sword it is."

"Mrs. Merryweather, you must have hurt yourself," Gretna cried.

She helped her up the stairs as best she could and across the landing to the room where they had washed their hands before. Now there was a fire lit in the grate and the communicating door was open to show another room, almost as large and magnificent, leading from it.

The housekeeper, who was supervising a warming-pan being put into the large four-poster, turned as they entered.

"I do not think Mrs. Merryweather is well," Gretna told her.

Instantly the woman forgot her airs and graces and became solicitous and understanding.

"Come and sit down," she said, helping Mrs. Merryweather through the communicating door into the other room. "The couch in here is more comfortable. Put your feet up and loosen your corsets. I expect it's the shock."

"She is complaining of a pain," Gretna said. "It is below the heart. I am wondering if she has cracked a rib. We were thrown quite violently on to the floor and I fell on Mrs. Merryweather, so I was not hurt."

"That's what it is dearie," Mrs. Merryweather groaned. "I remember hitting the side of the seat. That's what it is, I've busted one of my ribs. Here's a nice to-do."

"It will have to be strapped up," the housekeeper said. "Uncomfortable and painful it may be, but not dangerous. The gentlemen often have it happen out hunting. But you must keep quiet while we fetch the physician, and move as little as possible. Amy and Rose will help you undress."

"Lordy, Lordy!" Mrs. Merryweather exclaimed. "But I can't go to bed. I've got to look after Miss . . . I mean my niece."

"I can look after myself," Gretna said. "I promise you I can. Dear Mrs. Merryweather, you are not to worry."

"You cannot do a thing until you are strapped up," the housekeeper said in a voice of authority. "I will send one of the grooms for the physician right away, but he lives at Bridgewater and it will take an hour or so to fetch him. You must get into bed and wait for him. It is the only thing to do, I assure you."

"That is good advice," Gretna said.

Mrs. Merryweather compressed her lips. It was obvious

not only that she was in pain, but also that it was difficult for her to say anything more in front of the housekeeper and the chambermaids.

Only when finally they had got her into bed, dressed in a white muslin nightgown which the housekeeper had produced, did she lie back against the pillows and look at Gretna with consternation on her kind fat face.

"A fine tangle I've made of it," she said. "Now, harken to me, Miss Gretna. You are to say you want to dine up here with me. No going downstairs."

Gretna glanced over her shoulder to where, through the open door, she could see the housemaid unpacking one of her boxes which had just arrived. She could see her white muslin dress—the only new one she had had in five years, but which she had made specially for her journey to London—being taken out and shaken free of its creases. Just for a moment she hesitated, wishing to please Mrs. Merryweather. And then there was a dancing light in her eyes as she said:

"Pray forgive me, but I do want to go downstairs to dinner. I want to see the silver, I want to see the treasures that his Lordship has promised to show me."

Mrs. Merryweather groaned.

"Your poor mother would turn in her grave. You know as well as I do that you ought not to be dining alone with a gentleman."

"It will not matter because he has no idea who I am," Gretna answered. "I am not a Society miss to be chaperoned and cosseted. I am just an ordinary girl—your niece from a farm—that makes it quite all right, doesn't it?"

Mrs. Merryweather groaned again.

"You don't know what you are talking about, you silly child. You are to stay up here I tell you. Stay with me. I won't have you going down there. His Lordship is not the sort of person who . . . who you should be dining with."

"What sort of person is he then?" Gretna enquired. "Have you remembered what it was you had heard about him? Do tell me."

"I can't remember, that I can't," Mrs. Merryweather replied. "And yet somehow his name rings a bell—the Marquis of Stade. Someone was speaking of him. Maybe it was one of the huntsmen. They drop in after a day's hunting and talk about Society people. Maybe they said something about him. But whoever it is—it doesn't matter if what they said was good or bad—you don't dine downstairs alone with him. It ain't proper."

"What does it matter just for once?" Gretna pleaded. "Who is going to know? I shall never see him again; and if I do, I do not believe he would hold it against me. After all, it cannot be helped that you are ill."

"I could kick myself, I could really," Mrs. Merryweather said. "Why should a thing like this happen to me?" She glanced at the clock on the mantelpiece. "Perhaps the physician will be here. Perhaps I will be well enough to get up."

Gretna bent forward and kissed her on the forehead.

"Even if he comes in the next five minutes, he will not let you get up. You have got to rest, you know that."

She turned away before Mrs. Merryweather could say anything more, and, walking through the open door into her own bedroom, she saw that the maid had unpacked everything that was necessary for the night.

For the first time she was ashamed of her belongings—the thin, threadbare wrapper which had been washed and washed until it had long lost its original colour; the little worn slippers which had been hers since she was a child; the plain wooden hairbrush; her cotton petticoats, darned neatly but unornamented with embroidery or lace. They were all laid out for her, only her gown was missing. She guessed that the chambermaid had taken it away to have it pressed.

Yet when finally she was dressed and had arranged her hair as neatly and elegantly as she knew how, none of these things seemed to matter. She looked at herself in the mirror and was not ashamed of her appearance. The crisp white muslin might not compare with the elegant satin gowns that Society ladies wore on such occasions, but at least it was fresh and new.

To Gretna its very newness was a delight. The muslin had only cost a few shillings and she had made it up herself, for she had felt she could not go to London without one new gown in which she would not be ashamed to appear for the first time. There was a blue sash for her waist. It had been one of her mother's. It was over twenty years old and yet it looked as fresh and as pretty as the dress it ornamented.

A soft fichu framed the whiteness of her neck. For one moment she wished she had pearls to wear or even a little brooch of diamonds. And then she laughed at herself. Such ornamentation was not for her and not likely to be.

She was certain that her life in London would be very quiet. And yet, perhaps, sometimes she would get a chance of seeing ladies in their jewels and finery. It was so exciting to think that tomorrow she would be looking out on streets filled with traffic instead of just green fields with nothing more exciting moving amongst them than a cow or a goat.

And tonight—tonight was exciting too. She felt herself tremble a little in anticipation of what lay ahead of her. The Marquis was a frightening person, but it would be interesting to listen to him, to hear him talking, to realise that the gentlemen whom her mother had known when she was a girl had looked like him and lived in such grandeur.

Whatever Mrs. Merryweather might say, she would not miss it for anything in the world. Gretna gave one last look at herself in the mirror. She slipped into the room next door.

"I must go downstairs," she said. "It is time for dinner."

"Don't go, dearie! I beg of you, don't go!" Mrs. Merryweather begged.

"I can look after myself," Gretna replied, her head held high.

"You look about as much capable of that as a chicken who has just come out of the egg," Mrs. Merryweather snapped. And then she smiled. "Oh, well, I can quite understand you wanting to have a look at life. The Lord knows you've been quiet enough all these years, and I'm here if you want me. It isn't as if I wasn't in the house, is it?"

It was almost as if she was pleading for reassurance. Gretna bent forward and kissed her cheek.

"You are not to worry," she said reassuringly. "Just lie quietly until the physician comes, and I will come in to see if you are comfortable when I come up to bed."

"You won't be late?" Mrs. Merryweather insisted.

Gretna shook her head.

"Not a moment later than ten o'clock. I am persuaded that is the proper time for a correct young lady to retire!"

She moved from the room, conscious that despite the poor quality of her petticoats they rustled faintly round her feet. Then she opened the door of her bedroom. The light from the tapers in the great hall cast a golden glow over the landing.

She took a deep breath. This was like walking into a tremendous adventure. She was about to dine alone with a Marquis, a man she had never seen before today, but who was undoubtedly a personage of great importance and distinction.

Slowly she descended the stairs, playing a little game, with herself that she was wearing a gown of richly embroidered satin, that there were diamonds round her neck and her hair was powdered. She was not an ordinary country girl going down the stairs in her muslin. She was a queen, a princess, someone in a fairy-story, taking part in a great drama which was just beginning to unfold.

She felt herself thrill to her own imagination. She felt her heart beat a little quicker because she was excited; the breath come quicker between her lips.

And then, as she reached the bottom step, she realised that the Marquis had been watching her, standing in front of the fireplace, his hands behind him, his dark head tilted back a little to watch her come, the expression on his face inscrutable, his lips twisted in that strange, cynical smile.

2

AS DINNER ENDED and the footmen, in their gold-and-claret livery and powdered hair, left the room, the Marquis pushed back his chair a little and turning to Gretna said:

"Now, tell me about yourself."

The meal they had just eaten had seemed to Gretna almost unreal. Delicacies such as she had never heard of, let alone tasted, were provided in almost bewildering succession on gold plates. The dining-table was decorated with orchids and the huge candelabra which each held a dozen tapers, showed walls covered with valuable pictures.

It was, however, not the luxuriousness of her surroundings which made Gretna feel shy, but her host, with his strange, disconcerting smile and a manner of looking at her which she felt was always critical and frequently disdainful.

He looked as magnificent as the room he owned. His blue velvet coat was cut by a master hand; and though he was unpowdered, his hair was swept from his square forehead in the fashion sponsored by the Prince of Wales and tied at the neck with a ribbon.

There were diamonds glittering at his neck and on the buckles of his knee breeches, so that she was instantly aware of the plain inadequacies of her simple, cheap muslin gown. But because this was an adventure she refused to be downcast by her own appearance. What did it matter how she looked when tomorrow she would be gone and perhaps never again be privileged to see such splendour as was found here in Stade Hall?

She was more afraid that she would have little to talk about; but the Marquis, with a polished ease, led the conversation easily and without difficulty all during the course of dinner. He told her, among other things, that he had just recently returned from abroad.

"I had forgotten," he said, "how beautiful the English countryside can be in the spring."

"There is something exciting about April and May, is there not?" Gretna agreed. "One moment everything is bare, branches etched against the sky as if someone has drawn them in pen and ink. And then suddenly everything is green and gold. A few weeks ago the daffodils seemed to cover the garden at home. Now the lilacs are purple and white and the apple trees a cloud of blossom."

The Marquis gave her a curious glance; but as he did not question her further about her home, Gretna felt he was disinterested until, suddenly, the question she had been instinctively dreading came from his lips.

". . . tell me about yourself."

"There is . . . nothing to tell," she said a little hesitantly. "Unlike you, my Lord, I have lived a . . . very quiet life."

"Where?" he asked.

"Near Winchester," she replied.

"With your parents?"

"My father died nearly eighteen months ago; my mother last November. She did not wish to remain in this world after he had gone."

"They were fond of each other then?"

"They loved each other completely and absolutely." Gretna answered. "Life apart was intolerable and so my mother pined away, just counting the hours until she could be with my father again."

"And she did not mind leaving you?"

"I think she minded, but I was of little import beside the fact that she believed that she would be with my father again."

She felt that the Marquis might say something cynical, and stiffened. But instead he remarked in a voice that was almost kindly:

"So, you are all alone? Except, of course, for your aunt."

"My aunt?" Gretna queried, and then remembered Mrs. Merryweather. "Yes . . . yes . . . of course."

She wondered whether she should tell him the truth now that they were alone together, then Mrs. Merryweather's words of warning kept her silent. It was ridiculous, of course, and her instinct told her to take no notice of such croakings. At the same time, common sense whispered that it was wisest to play safe rather than take a chance.

"And what do you plan to do in London?" the Marquis asked.

"I plan to stay with . . . a friend for a time. Someone I have known all my life."

"Will she find you employment, do you think? I gather that your parents have not left you well off."

"No, indeed," Gretna answered. "I have not a penny to bless myself with That is why I am going to London."

The Marquis rested his chin on his hand and watched the exquisite little face turned towards his. The eyes, surprisingly blue in the light of the candles, were so expressive that it seemed to him that he could see the thoughts mirrored in them almost before the words came to the full red lips.

"What can you do?" he asked, his voice surprisingly deep. "What is there in London for anyone like you to do?"

"I do not know yet," Gretna answered. "Maybe I could be a companion to an old lady; perhaps I could teach children."

Her face darkened as she spoke and she thought how frightening it would be to go to an unknown house, to be at a stranger's beck and call, to strive to please an employer who might be too exacting or demand more than she was capable of giving.

The Marquis, watching her, thought that it was unlikely that any sensible woman would employ anyone so pretty as a governess. As for being a companion, what a fate for a Nymph of Spring to be tied to the side of old and disgruntled Winter.

"I think you are over-young for such positions," he said at length.

"Oh, no," Gretna contradicted. "I shall be eighteen next October. I know other girls start far earlier than that to earn a living."

The Marquis, watching her, seemed to be cogitating something in his mind, but after a short silence he rose to his feet and suggested that they repair to the Salon. Gretna rose in confusion.

"Oh dear!" she exclaimed. "Ought I to have withdrawn and left you to your port? Mamma has told me that that was what the ladies should do at a party. I am afraid I forgot. We have never had any port in our house for so long. Papa liked it, but the doctor forbade it after he became so ill."

The Marquis looked a little puzzled, wondering what sort of farmer it was who liked a glass of port with his supper. But he said nothing, only followed Gretna's outspread muslin skirts towards the Salon.

A footman, however, showed her not into the large room where she had sat on arrival, but into a smaller room opening out of it—a cosy, comfortable little anteroom with curtains of exquisite tapestry and walls partially covered with shelves on which was arranged a fine collection of Chelsea china and Battersea enamel.

Gretna gave an exclamation at their beauty, and then another cry of delight because, lying on the hearth in front of the fire, were two black-and-white spaniels. They allowed her to caress them, pushing their cold noses against her little hands and looking with melting eyes first at her and then at their master.

"Do not encourage them," the Marquis said. "They are incorrigibly sentimental and always greedy for affection."

"Are we not all like that?" Gretna asked, smiling up at him.

She had no idea of the picture she made, half kneeling on the hearthrug, the spaniels close against her, her golden head silhouetted against a chair upholstered in ruby velvet.

The Marquis stood looking at her for a moment and

then settled himself in a wing-backed chair on the other side of the hearthrug.

"I wonder what will become of you?" he mused aloud.

"I often wonder that myself," Gretna said artlessly. "To tell you the truth, I am a little afraid. London seems so big, so frightening when one thinks about it. But I shall be with my friend. I am sure she will permit me to stay with her until I can find employment."

"Have you known her a long time?"

"Ever since I was born," Gretna answered.

"Perhaps you will permit me to call and see you one day."

He noticed the hesitation before Gretna replied, and wondered why she dropped her eyes from his, obviously intent on making a fuss of one of the spaniels. He could not guess that once again she was wondering whether to tell the truth, to explain who she was. It seemed, she thought, so ungracious to go on deceiving him when he was so kind. And then she remembered that, if he knew the truth about her, there then would be the embarrassment that she should not have been dining alone with him unchaperoned.

Because he believed her a niece of dear, fat, kind Mrs. Merryweather upstairs, because he believed that she came of farmers' stock, then the conventions could be disregarded and no one feel the worse for their absence.

As if such thoughts brought Mrs. Merryweather's suffering to her mind, Gretna looked up suddenly.

"I wonder if the physician has been?" she said.

"I will enquire," the Marquis answered. He rang the bell and told the footman who answered it to make enquiries immediately.

The man had hardly left the room before his place was taken by the butler.

"The physician has just left, m'Lord. He asked me to inform your Lordship that the lady, while suffering from bruises and shock, has broken no bones. He has given her a sleeping draught and she should be quite well enough to travel in the morning."

"That is splendid news," Gretna cried, clasping her hands together. "I was so worried lest she had really cracked a rib, as the housekeeper thought."

The butler withdrew and the Marquis said:

"I am glad your aunt is no worse, but sorry that there is now no excuse for me to press you into staying a little longer. Perhaps in the morning you might care to consider an invitation to linger here for a day or two."

"I would like it above all things," Gretna said softly. "This house is so lovely! But my friend will be expecting me in London."

"In that case I must not try and divert your plans," the Marquis said.

He sounded almost relieved, she thought, and wondered if he had given her the invitation impulsively and then regretted it. She peeped up at him from under her eyelashes. How grim and uncompromising he could look, she thought, when he was not speaking. It was almost as if he was nice in spite of himself.

He was looking into the fire. She thought that in repose his mouth was cruel. He could be hard and very imperative if he wished. She felt herself shiver a little as if the thought of his anger had the power to disturb her. And then, suddenly, the look was gone and he was smiling at her.

"I am still trying to think how I can help you," he said. "And wondering if amongst my many relations there is not someone who could offer you employment more congenial than that of governess or companion. The trouble, my dear, is that you are far too pretty."

"Too pretty!" Gretna echoed, and then her face seemed to light up. "Do you really think so? No one has told me that before—except Papa. Long ago before he was so ill, he used to call me his sunbeam. But then, one can hardly credit all that one's father says, can one?"

"Not all," the Marquis agreed with a twist of his lips.,

"Do you think that perhaps, if I had nice clothes, if I had my hair dressed in a fashionable manner, I should look like some of the ladies whom one hears about in London? So beautiful; so elegant. Could I look like them, do you think?"

The Marquis's expression darkened.

"God forbid you should do so!" he said. "Remain as you are—unspoilt, untainted by what is called Society."

He spoke harshly and added sternly:

"Do not play with fire! The social world is not for you. Go back to the country and make some honest farmer happy."

Gretna bent her head to hide the disappointment in her eyes. She almost felt as if he had struck her, mocking her aspirations, making her feel a fool for what she had said.

And then, as if her chagrin communicated itself to him, he suddenly put out his hand.

"Come here, child," he said.

She half rose to obey him, slipping her little fingers into his and feeling the sudden warmth and strength of the hand that grasped them. He drew her a little nearer and now she was beside him, half kneeling at his feet, her face turned up towards his, her hair-curls seeming to halo her head, her eyes a little troubled, her mouth drooping a little as if she were still smarting from the blow he had given her.

"Gretna!" the Marquis said, and his voice was low. "I think we were fated to meet today. Do you feel that too?"

"I . . . I do not know," Gretna stammered.

"You are so young and so helpless," he said, speaking almost beneath his breath. "What will London do to you? Is it wise or right of me to permit you to go there?"

"Permit me?" Gretna questioned in surprise.

"Supposing I made another proposition to you?" the Marquis asked. "Supposing I suggested that I should look after you?"

"But . . . I do not . . . understand," Gretna answered.

"Shall I explain?" the Marquis asked, his eyes on hers.

He still clasped her hand, her eyes were held by his. She felt as if something strange and alive passed between them, she felt herself suddenly tremble. She did not know what it was, but it was as if something tingled through her whole body, making her breath come a little quicker from between her parted lips, the colour rising very slowly in her pale cheeks.

She could not move, she could not speak. She could only stare at him, stare into the impenetrable depths of those dark eyes which seemed to hold her, and then change and deepen until she fancied, for one unbelievable moment, that she saw a fire deep down in them.

She wanted to run away and she wanted to stay. She wanted to move, but she could only remain where she was. She could not think, she could not understand. She could only feel—feel something strange happening to her and, not understanding what it was, knew that her whole body responded.

And then, while she waited, while she could not even breathe, the door was suddenly opened. The butler crossed the room and the Marquis let go of Gretna's hand. She sat back on her heels, her arms went round one of the spaniels and, dropping her head, she laid her cheek against its soft, silky coat.

"What is it?"

The Marquis's voice was harsh.

"Lord Wroxhall has called, m'Lord."

"Lord Wroxhall!"

"Yes, m'Lord. He wishes to speak with your Lordship and I have shown him into the Salon."

"Very good. I will join him there."

The Marquis rose to his feet. He looked down for a moment at Gretna, her face hidden, her pale gold curls falling in sweet confusion over her shoulders.

"Wait here," he said. "I will not be long."

He left the room, going into the Salon which adjoined it, not by the door through which the butler had come but by another smaller door placed in the corner of the room where it could scarcely be noticed.

He shut the door behind him, and now that she was sure he had gone Gretna raised her head and looked after him. Very slowly her two hands crept up towards her cheeks. What had happened? Why did she feel like this? What strange effect was it that he had upon her? She was afraid of him and yet, at the same time, she thought that she trusted him.

"When he returns, I will tell him the truth about myself," she thought, and knew that because of what had happened in that moment she wanted to sweep away all pretence and deception.

What did he mean by what he had suggested? Would he personally find her employment? Did he mean here at Stade Hall? she wondered, but could find no answer to her questions. He would explain when he returned she thought happily.

She felt a movement beside her and saw one of the spaniels rise and look in the direction in which his master had gone and then trot resolutely towards the door. He found it shut, whined and then pressed against it. It could not have been properly latched because it opened a crack and the spaniel inserted his nose, then his head and finally his body disappeared completely.

It was then that Gretna heard the Marquis's voice. For a moment she just listened to his deep tones, hearing it as a sound rather than because the words he was speaking made any sense. And then she heard another man's voice. It drawled and yet had an oily quality about it.

"The Prince could hardly credit you had returned and not been to see him."

"I have only been back in England for three weeks and there has been much for me to do here."

"Your friends in London will not feel complimented by your reluctance to greet them."

"I have little anxiety to do so, if it comes to that."

"Really, Julien," Lord Wroxhall exclaimed. "You can hardly expect me to credit that sentiment unless, of course, you are still wearing the willow for Eloise. Buckhurst remains her protector as you know."

"Eloise's life or her associations are not of the slightest interest to me," the Marquis said, and his tone was icy.

Lord Wroxhall laughed.

"Doing it a bit brown, aren't you, Julien? We all knew you must have been mad as fire that Eloise did not accompany you into exile. Oh, well! Such women are all the same."

"You are right," the Marquis agreed. "But you do not go far enough. All women are the same—selfish, greedy, wanting all they can get out of a man and determined to give as little as possible in return."

"And yet the world would be a dead bore without them," Lord Wroxhall said. "And certainly the Prince would find it so."

"Tell me, how is His Royal Highness?" the Marquis enquired.

"Well enough in health, but he is just as irresponsible and impetuous as he has ever been. You have heard about his latest of course?"

"No, I have heard nothing," the Marquis said. "Strangely enough, in Hungary—for that is where I have been—the *scandale* of the *beau monde* are not of the least consequence."

"Then what the devil did you talk about?"

"Horses mostly," the Marquis said. "And sometimes of even more serious subjects. But those, my dear Wroxhall, would not interest you or the *beau monde*."

Although Gretna could not see Lord Wroxhall, she sensed that he shrugged his shoulders.

" 'Pon rep, Julien, sneer as you please! I cannot say I envy you. The wilderness was never for me. Ah, well! So you haven't heard."

"Heard what?"

"What everyone is saying. The latest *on dit* about the Prince."

"What is it?"

"Well, quite a number of people are absolutely convinced that he has married Maria Fitzherbert."

"That is impossible!"

"So Charles Fox avers, but others are sure that a marriage ceremony has taken place."

"Do you really know what you are saying?" the Marquis asked. "Just before I went abroad last year Mrs. Fitzherbert had left for France, swearing she would have none of the Prince and his amorous philanderings. I do not know the woman but I understood that she had finished with him for good and all."

"That's what we all thought," Lord Wroxhall agreed. "But she returned last December—they say at the Prince's urgent invitation. The buzz round the clubs is that they were married soon after she arrived."

"You must have all taken leave of your senses!" the Marquis said angrily. "How could the Prince marry a Roman Catholic? How could anyone credit such a ridiculous, absurd, idiotic state of affairs in which the Prince would deliberately put his head into a noose of that kind? Parliament would not stand for it. The country would not stand for it. A Roman Catholic, Wroxhall! They may have received a few concessions lately, but they won't get any more."

"I am only telling you, Julien, what is being said. I am not saying, personally, whether it is true or untrue. I am only relating that a large number of people believe it to be a fact."

"Then the Carlton House set must be more bird-witted than usual," the Marquis said rudely.

"Well, you had best come and see for yourself. The Prince is asking for you and if he hasn't married the lady in question, then you may be able to prevent it."

"I'll prevent it," the Marquis said grimly, "if I have to shake some sense into the Prince. These damned scheming women are all the same. Perdita Robinson had a bond for twenty thousand guineas from him. And the King paid five thousand for her letters. And now this damned Roman Catholic is out to bleed him."

"She's a lady, Julien."

"Lady be damned! A Roman Catholic and a woman. Could there be a worse combination? If I have to throttle her with my own hands, I will stop her making a fool of the Prince. After all, he is little more than a boy."

"Then you will come to London?"

"I will come tomorrow. You can tell His Royal Highness that I will attend him at Carlton House after dinner."

"Best put it in writing," Lord Wroxhall said. "You know how the Prince enjoys formalities of that sort."

"I will write him a note," the Marquis agreed. "But if you have been foxing me, Wroxhall, I swear I will call you out for it."

"I vow that I have been telling you the truth," Lord Wroxhall replied suavely.

Gretna heard footsteps crossing the room and then a door slammed and she realised for the first time the feeling of guilt that she had been eavesdropping. It was not only that which made her cheeks so pale or her hands tremble visibly. She rose to her feet, wondering whether she should escape before the Marquis returned. Then, as she stood irresolute, the door that was half ajar between the rooms opened fully and she saw a man watching her.

"So this is what our friend Julien was hiding," he said softly in that drawling, oily voice which she had disliked from the first moment she had heard it.

She turned to face him. He was obviously a dandy, but yet his figure had never intended him to be one. He was a little hunched, his head thrust forward. He had glittering eyes beneath heavy, hooded eyelids, a thick sensuous mouth and hands that seemed a little too big for his body.

He came towards her, raising his quizzing glass to inspect her.

"A beauty!" he exclaimed. "A beauty indeed! So this is why Julien is no longer interested in the fair Eloise!"

He came nearer and Gretna felt that she could not move but only stand watching his progress towards her as if she was mesmerised. She hated the look in his eyes, his suggestive thick-lipped smile. Then, as he reached her, he put out a hand to touch her chin and she winced violently away from him.

"Nervous?" he asked. "A filly that has not been completely broken. Lucky Julien to be the breaker."

"I must ask you to excuse me, my Lord." Gretna hardly managed to whisper the words. She did not know why, but she was frightened and her heart was beating almost painfully.

She would have passed him and gone towards the door,

but, putting out a hand, he took her arm and the touch of his fingers made her shiver.

"Not so fast, not so fast," he said. "What is your name and where do you come from?"

" 'Tis of no consequence, my Lord."

"But it is," he answered. "The Marquis is a friend of mine and what interests him is always of interest to me. Tell me your name."

Gretna tried to move away from him, but he held her fast.

"My name is Gretna, my Lord," she said. "And now will you please let me go?"

"Gretna! A charming name. An unusual one. Were your parents married at Gretna Green?"

"Yes, my Lord."

"I might have guessed it. Something so beautiful could only have come from a runaway marriage or a liaison of great passion. But for your name I should have suspected you to be a love child."

Gretna drew herself up.

"I think, my Lord, you insult me."

"Of course not. Why should I do anything so stupid? I am only telling you how much I admire you. So much so that before your protector returns I am going to steal a kiss from that pretty red mouth of yours."

He pulled her towards him.

"No! Please no!"

Gretna struggled so violently that she broke away from him and running across the room stood with her back against the window, her arms, outstretched to clutch the curtains, her eyes wide with fear, her breasts moving tempestuously beneath the soft muslin of her gown.

"Gad, you're a beauty!" Lord Wroxhall ejaculated, and then he started to move slowly, inexorably towards her.

He was like a hunter stalking his prey and enjoying every moment of the chase. She knew it even as she stood hypnotised for one split second before she ran—speeding panic-stricken across the room to reach the door into the hall just as the Marquis opened it from the other side.

She flung herself against him, holding on to him, trembling violently in every limb and yet unable to say anything.

"What is this?"

The Marquis's question did not really require an answer. It was only too obvious what was happening, with

Lord Wroxhall moving across the room with a look on his face which no-one could mistake and Gretna's breath coming in gasps almost as if she was sobbing.

Slowly the Marquis put an arm around Gretna, then with the other hand he held out a note towards Lord Wroxhall.

"Take this and get out."

Lord Wroxhall took it, the smile still parting his lips, his eyes full of evil.

"Accept my congratulations, Julien," he said. "Your taste was always impeccable."

"Go back to London and stay there," the Marquis commanded.

"I will leave immediately," Lord Wroxhall replied. "I am well aware I am *de trop*. I can only apologise that I intruded at such an inopportune moment."

He paused and then looked at Gretna whose face was still hidden against the Marquis's shoulder.

"*Au revoir*, Miss Gretna," he said. "I trust, indeed I am sure, that we shall meet again."

He laughed once, a laugh without humour that was somehow sinister and, to Gretna's ears, terrifying. And then he was gone and the door closed behind him.

"Come and sit down," the Marquis said. "There is no need to be afraid."

He did not speak kindly, but with an icily repressed anger. His lips were in a tight hard line as he looked down at Gretna and his eyes were smouldering with rage.

With a tremendous effort Gretna managed to control the panic which still possessed her.

"I . . . I am sorry," she said, stammering a little. "He . . . he frightened me."

"So I understand," the Marquis said. "He shall be made to pay for it one day."

He moved across the room back to the fireplace where they had sat before.

"Come here," he commanded. "I apologise for the interruption. It was unfortunate that Lord Wroxhall should have called on this particular evening."

Gretna drew in her breath. She was remembering what she had overheard, what the Marquis had said in his conversation with Lord Wroxhall.

"I must retire," she said. "I must go upstairs and see if Mrs. Merryweather is asleep."

"There is no necessity," the Marquis said. "My physician is, I assure you, a very efficient one. As he has given her a sleeping draught, she will be asleep now until the morning. Sit down. We will continue our conversation where we left it."

"No, no, it is impossible," Gretna said.

"But, why?" he enquired.

"I am tired. I ask your permission, my Lord, to retire."

She knew he was angry at her refusal by the sudden coldness of his voice as he said:

"Very well, if that is your wish."

"Good night, my Lord, and thank you."

There was almost the distance of the room between them. She dropped him a curtsy and realised that he was about to move to open the door for her. She forestalled him by reaching it first, slipping outside into the hall and then running as hard as she could through the marble pillars and up the broad staircase to her bedchamber.

She shut the door behind her and locked herself in, turning the key and trying the handle to be quite certain it was locked. Then she dropped down on the hearthrug, throwing herself full length on the floor to hide her face in her arms.

Not to cry, but to think, to let the conversation beween the Marquis and Lord Wroxhall repeat and repeat itself in her mind until she thought she must go mad with listening to it.

3

"CAN I MAKE you more comfortable, dear Mrs. Merryweather?" Gretna asked.

"I'm all right, dearie. Don't you worrit your pretty head about me," Mrs. Merryweather replied, settling herself in a corner of the stage-coach. "I just can't think how I came to make such a ninny of myself. When the physician said that nothing was broken, I could have cried out of sheer vexation."

"He said you were terribly bruised and suffering from shock," Gretna answered soothingly.

"Shock, indeed! It takes an old fool of my age to be

upset by a little thing like that. But he was right when he said I was bruised. I'm coming out black and blue from top to toe. I shall look like the tattooed woman at the circus by the time I've finished."

Mrs. Merryweather chuckled in her usual rich, warm manner and then the sound turned to a little groan.

"Bust my laces, but I feel as if a dozen horses had driven over me."

"You will have to take things quietly for a day or two," Gretna advised.

"Much chance of that with you getting me out of bed as the cock crowed and hurrying me down here as if the very fiends in hell were after us. What happened last night?"

Mrs. Merryweather turned a pair of searching eyes upon Gretna. There was a noticeable hesitation before the latter replied.

"Nothing, I assure you . . . b . . . but I knew you were in a hurry to get to St. Albans and I . . . am consumed by the urgency to arrive in London."

"The Marquis—— he treated you—— properly?" Mrs. Merryweather asked in a conspiratorial stage whisper.

"But of course."

Gretna's chin went a little higher as if the suggestion was impudent.

"Now, you mustn't mind me asking, dearie," Mrs. Merryweather said apologetically. "I feel responsible to the memory of your blessed mother. It was not right that a lady in your position should dine alone with a gentleman—least of all the Marquis, whatever airs and graces he may give himself."

"There is no reason for your concern," Gretna replied with a little edge on her voice as if she had no wish to speak further of what had occurred.

"Then wherefore the haste?" Mrs. Merryweather asked. "An hour we've had to wait till these lazy good-for-nothing coachmen could stir their stumps and get the horses between the shafts. Why the hurry if there's no reason behind it?"

"I wanted to get to . . . to London," Gretna answered simply.

Mrs. Merryweather pressed her lips together. It was quite obvious that she was not satisfied. At the same time, she was not in a position to press her curiosity further.

The stage-coach was jogging along at a comfortable

pace, but even so the movement was giving her pain. But she forgot her own aches in watching Gretna's averted face and puzzling as to what had happened the night before.

The girl was looking definitely pale, Mrs. Merryweather decided. Not that such a pallor was unbecoming, in fact it gave her a fragile, almost spiritual air which somehow accentuated her beauty. But there were dark lines under her eyes as if she had not slept and her pretty mouth was drooping at the corners a little wistfully. In fact, there was something in her whole manner that told Mrs. Merryweather that she was troubled.

They travelled in silence, Mrs. Merryweather cogitating over what she had heard and trying to make up her mind what was the best approach to find out more. Suddenly Gretna turned to her and in a tone that was almost one of anguish, asked:

"You are sure, Mrs. Merryweather, that I am doing what is right in going to London to Aunt Maria?"

Mrs. Merryweather stared at her in surprise. This was a question she had not expected.

"Why, bless my soul," she exclaimed, "where else would you go? You know she's always said that you could rely on her if anything happened to your mother. I've heard her myself a thousand times."

"Then why didn't she answer my letter that I wrote to her when Mamma died?"

"She was abroad, dearie. And you know what the posts are in those outlandish places—Aix-la-Chapelle, or whatever it was called. Ten to one she never got the letter."

"But I have not seen her for such a long time—over two years—perhaps she will have forgotten about me."

Mrs. Merryweather gave a big laugh which seemed to come right from within the depths of her fat stomach, and then stifled it with an ejaculation of pain.

"Forget about you? Why dearie, you know as well as I do that Mistress Fitzherbert has always doted upon you. 'My baby', she used to call you when you were little. I can see her now coming to the cottage just after you were born. I was in the sitting-room tidying up. She comes running in through the door; she must have been twelve at the time. As pretty a picture as you could see anywhere."

Mrs. Merryweather smiled at the memory before she continued:

" 'Where is the baby, Mrs. Merry?' she cried. That was

what she always called me. It was a sort of joke between us because I was always joking. 'Upstairs, Miss' I says to her, 'and don't you go waking her either.' She runs upstairs two at a time and then I hear her knocking ever so softly on your mother's door. She was always considerate of other people's feelings was Miss Maria."

"And what did she say after that?" Gretna asked, not because she hadn't heard the story a thousand times before but because it was somehow comforting.

"She comes downstairs looking as solemn as an owl," Mrs. Merryweather said. " 'And what do you think of her, Miss?' I asks. 'She's lovely, Mrs. Merry! She's lovely! I shall come and see her every day and make her my very own baby.' She kept her word right enough!"

"Every day?" Gretna asked.

"Come rain, come shine," Mrs. Merryweather answered, "she'd come in to see you. Sometimes she'd only be able to stay a moment or two, but sure enough she'd never miss. She's older now, but her feelings haven't changed. Why, the very last time I saw her—it must have been just about two years ago—that was it . . . May, 1784—she says to me, 'Mrs Merry, look after Miss Gretna and her Ladyship, and if anything happens or they should want anything, you are to let me know.' Your father was ill at that time and we were all afraid her Ladyship would break down under the strain of nursing him."

"I still cannot think why she did not write to me when Mamma died," Gretna worried.

"I'm as certain sure as I'm sitting here she never got the letter. I know she's in London now. They told me up at the big house that she came back in December and they gave me the address—Park Street, wasn't it?"

"That's right, Park Street, Park Lane," Gretna said.

"Then you can be sure you will find her waiting for you."

"I wish I could have had an answer to my last letter—the one I wrote three days ago telling her I was coming to her in London."

"Well, there wasn't time, was there?" Mrs. Merryweather asked. "With that horrible bailiff taking the cottage off you and saying it wasn't decent that you should be living there alone. Decent, indeed! You wait till Mr. Walter Smythe hears of this. He'll have something to say."

"He may never hear," Gretna said quietly.

"You mean he may die abroad?" Mrs. Merryweather

asked. "They don't give much for his chances up at the big house. The poor gentleman was ill, a very ill man when he went away. 'Tis strange that someone as active as he was attacked by the paralysis. But then, we none of us know what God has in store for us."

Mrs. Merryweather gave a heavy sigh.

"You could have come to me, dearie, as that rascally bailiff suggested."

"Oh, no, Mrs. Merryweather. You know I could not do that," Gretna said. "It would have meant turning Fred or Bill out of their room. It would not be fair when they work so hard. Besides, you have got quite enough to do without looking after me."

"Now let's get this fair and square," Mrs. Merryweather retorted. "There's always room for you, dearie, at the farm whatever happens. It may not be the proper sort of accommodation for the gentry, but there's always a place for you, just as there's always a place for you, bless your sweet face, in my heart."

"Oh, Mrs. Merryweather, you are so kind to me," Gretna answered, pressing her hand. "And I know you made the excuse to go and see your sister in St. Albans just so that you could accompany me on this journey. I am grateful, I am really."

"Don't you go talking such nonsense," Mrs. Merryweather admonished. "A nice thing it would be if I couldn't do something for you after working for your blessed mother and your dear father all these years. I admired both of them, that I did, and as for you, I loved you from the very moment I clapped eyes on you. All I want is you to be happy and to be brought up in the sort of society to which you are entitled. Living alone in that poky little cottage or hanging about at the farm with no-one to talk to isn't right. No, dearie, Miss Maria—I beg her pardon, Mistress Fitzherbert, will do what is right for you."

"I hope so. I hope so, indeed," Gretna answered. "But somehow she seems so far away, so very grown up and out of reach."

"Bless my soul, you mustn't be thinking like that. She's had her troubles, has Miss Maria. Losing two husbands before she was twenty-five is bound to leave its mark on any woman. And she was so happy with Mr. Fitzherbert, for all he was ten years older than herself."

"But her first husband was older still, wasn't he?"

"Indeed, he was! Oh, that Mr. Weld, I never did hold

with that marriage. Twenty-six years older than his bride and she but a girl of eighteen. And it seems as if I was right in saying he was not suitable, for God took him to his rest the very same year as they were married."

"And now? Whom do you . . . think Aunt Maria loves now?"

The words came out hesitantly and Gretna did not look at Mrs. Merryweather as she spoke.

"Well, there'll be gentlemen enough wanting to marry her, you may be sure of that," came the answer. "She always had a way with her. She could charm anyone. Old or young, they all fell for Miss Maria. It wasn't only that she was pretty, it was something in her manner, in her voice. Gentle as a dove she could be and as sweet as honey in the honeycomb."

"Do you think there is . . . any particular gentleman?"

"If there is, I ain't heard of him," Mrs. Merryweather replied. "But then, Miss Maria always liked living quietly. She never cared for Society or racketing around with all those noisy young bloods. I've heard Agnes, her old maid, talk about her friends and say what nice people came to her house when she was married to Mr. Fitzherbert. No card parties or routs for her. What she really preferred was to be sitting at her embroidery or driving out in her carriage to take the air."

"Then any rumours that she has changed and that she is living a very . . . different life would be untrue, wouldn't they?" Gretna asked.

"Of course they would," Mrs. Merryweather said quickly, and added: "What have you been hearing? Who's been talking? Don't tell me that Marquis was a-gossiping about Mistress Fitzherbert. Did you tell him you were visiting her?"

"No, of course not," Gretna replied quickly. "He thought I was your niece."

"It's sorry I am that I ever said such a thing," Mrs. Merryweather remarked. " 'Twould have been best to tell the truth. But I had to think quickly and it seemed a good idea at the time. Now I'm certain sure it was a mistake."

"Oh, no, you were right," Gretna cried. "It would have been terrible if you had mentioned Aunt Maria to the Marquis."

"Terrible! Why's that?"

"Oh, no . . . no . . . r . . . reason."

Gretna would say no more, however hard Mrs. Merryweather tried to find out what she meant by such a remark or what had happened the night before. The good lady was very perplexed and yet there was nothing she could do about it.

They arrived in London and were set down at the posting-house. Mrs. Merryweather found a hackney carriage to carry Gretna to Park Street before she hurried to catch her own coach to St. Albans.

Gretna hugged her as they said good-bye.

"Thank you, dear, dear Mrs. Merryweather, for all you have done for me," she said. "I can never be sufficiently grateful and I will write to you and tell you all about everything, I promise you that."

"Now, you look after yourself, dearie. I shall be thinking of you, praying for you too, but I know you will be all right with Miss Maria. And please to give her my respects."

"I will, indeed," Gretna promised, and waved good-bye from the hackney carriage as it drove away, leaving Mrs. Merryweather staring after her with a troubled expression on her kind, fat face.

Gretna settled herself in the corner of the carriage, then opened her purse to be quite certain she had enough money to pay the fare. Now she was alone, all the questions and problems that had been troubling her the night before came rushing back with renewed violence to make an onslaught on her mind and serenity.

Could it be true what she had overheard? That the Prince of Wales was in love with Aunt Maria? Mistress Fitzherbert was not really an aunt, but ever since Maria Smythe had 'adopted' her as a baby—as Mrs. Merryweather would so often recall—she had looked up to her, loved her and eventually the relationship had been formulated into that of "aunt and niece."

Gretna was only five when Maria first married and it would not have been correct for her to call a married woman by her christian name and so Maria became "Aunt Maria". Later, as Mistress Fitzherbert, she swore no one could have a more devoted relative.

"You are my little girl, aren't you, Gretna?" she asked once as she had held her in a close embrace and accepted the buttercups which Gretna had picked for her in the meadows outside the cottage door.

"Of course I am," Gretna replied. "But why do you not have a little girl of your own just like me?"

Both Mistress Fitzherbert and her mother had laughed, but Gretna had seen the pain on Aunt Maria's face and been intuitive enough never to mention her childless state to her again.

What had Lord Wroxhall meant when he said that a number of people believed that the Prince of Wales had married her? Gretna might be innocent, she might have lived out of the world, but she was a Protestant and she was well aware from her close association with Mistress Fitzherbert's parents. Mr. and Mrs. Walter Smythe, that Roman Catholics had a very difficult time.

Deprived of their civil rights, treated as aliens and suspects in the land of their birth, they were forced to practise their religion almost by stealth. Their priests lived in fear, and their chapels were bolted before the Mass to keep out spies.

Maria's two brothers, John and Frederick, were not allowed to enter the Army or Navy. They were in fact debarred from holding any form of position under the Crown.

How often Gretna had heard her father and mother say how unfair their position was and that it was not surprising that the two young men were very wild in consequence. Their father, Mr. Walter Smythe, had held a commission in the Austrian Army and finally John had gone abroad and enlisted, much to the distress and unhappiness of his parents.

"I think our treatment of the Catholics in this country is monstrously unfair!"

Gretna could hear her mother saying that in her soft, sweet voice, but with her eyes a little fiery as they were when she heard of injustice and cruelty.

"I know, my dearest," her husband replied. "But there has been so much religious trouble in the past that Parliament has done its best to stamp out religious differences by preventing the Catholics from getting into any position from which they could antagonise their compatriots."

"I should have thought," Gretna's mother said angrily, "that treating them as we do was just the way to cause not only unhappiness but differences, arguments and even revolution."

"Hush, hush, Rosemary. I cannot allow you to say such sentiments aloud. It is almost treason."

"Then I will be treasonable," his wife said, her pretty head held high. "When I think how kind the Smythes are, what good friends they have been to us, then I am prepared to fight their battles and support their cause even if it means defying the King himself."

Gretna could still hear her mother's challenge. She could remember so well how her father picked up his wife's hand and kissed it.

"You were always braver than I, my love," he said softly.

It was true, indeed, that Mr. and Mrs. Walter Smythe had been kind to Captain William Hayden and his family. It was many years before Gretna realised how much they owed to the quiet Roman Catholic family. But when she was a child, she was well aware of the great hampers of fruit and vegetables that arrived once a week at the little cottage in the village from Brambridge Hall. There was game, too, at the right season of the year—pheasants, partridges and even sometimes a haunch of venison.

But when she was old enough to understand, Gretna learned of other things which had forged a link between the Smythe family and her own. One day she asked her mother why she was called Gretna.

"People always say to me, 'What a funny name!' Mamma."

"It is a strange name for a child," her mother admitted. "But you were called Gretna because your father and I were married at Gretna Green. It is a place where lovers go when they run away to get married."

"Tell me all about it," Gretna begged, and her mother related the whole romantic story of the blacksmith's forge, of the wild rush across the border, a wedding ring thrust on with trembling fingers while the bridegroom glanced hastily over his shoulder to see if the pursuing carriages were in sight.

"So you were married like that!" Gretna exclaimed. "How wonderful! But why? Why couldn't you have been married at home?"

Her mother's face was suddenly overshadowed. For a moment she had hesitated and then she said:

"I wonder if you are old enough to know the truth, Gretna? I have always meant to tell you my story one day. Somehow I still think of you as my baby, too young to know anything except that I love you."

"I am old enough, I am really, Mamma," Gretna pleaded.

"Very well," her mother answered, and taking a deep breath she said:

"Your grandfather was the Earl of Ledbury. He was a very strict and not a particularly kind father, and my mother always did exactly what he commanded. I was their only child and because your grandfather was a very rich man he spent a great deal of money when I made my début in presenting me at Court and giving me what was called the *entrée* into London Society."

"Oh, tell me about it. Tell me all about it," Gretna cried.

"I will tell you about the parties later," her mother promised. "For the moment I want to keep to the story as to why your father and I were married at Gretna Green."

"Yes, yes, of course," Gretna agreed, hardly able to breathe with the excitement of it.

"I had what I might almost call, without conceit, a success in London," her mother went on. "And there was no doubt at all that my father was proud of me. When the Duke of Avon proposed, he was delighted and accepted the offer of marriage on my behalf without even consulting me."

"Without even asking if you wanted to marry the Duke?" Gretna enquired.

"I was just told I was to be married," Lady Rosemary said, her voice suddenly a little frightened as if the memory of that dark hour came back to her all too vividly. "The Duke was not only much older than I, but the licentious, wicked life he had led had made him almost as repulsive in appearance as he was in character.

"He was a bad man, Gretna. I had known it from the very first moment I saw him and I had done my best to avoid him on the few occasions on which he had singled me out for his attentions. But his Grace was very rich. He was also a very powerful man and my father was quite right in saying it would have been, from the worldly point of view, a brilliant match for me."

"What did you do, Mamma?" Gretna asked.

"I could do nothing," Lady Rosemary answered. "My father announced that the wedding would take place in six months' time and my mother started to prepare my trousseau."

"Were your gowns very lovely?" Gretna enquired.

"Very magnificent," her mother answered. "But I hated every one of them—not only because of the long hours I had to stand fitting them but because I knew that they were to be worn for the delectation of a man whom I detested."

"Could you not have refused to marry him?" Gretna asked.

Her mother shook her head.

"In my home no-one refused to do anything if my father wished it."

"Then what did you do?" Gretna asked.

"It was during those six months when I was choosing my trousseau that I met your father. The very moment I set eyes on him I knew he was the one man whom I loved and whom I should always love, and he felt the same way about me."

"Did he tell you so?" Gretna asked.

"Not at once. No, he tried to behave honourably, to go away, to avoid seeing me again. But fate flung us together."

Lady Rosemary gave a little sigh and then a smile lit her face as if it were a lamp shining through the clouds.

"I shall never forget when we first admitted that we loved each other. And I was desperate when your father told me that the only decent thing he could do was to go away and never see me again. But he was not strong enough, thank God, to do that."

"And what did you do?" Gretna enquired. "What did you do, Mamma?"

"I did the one unforgivable, the one terrible thing that I ought never to have done," Lady Rosemary answered. "I hithered and hathered and was too frightened to make up my mind until the very night before my wedding. Everything was arranged for a magnificent ceremony at St. George's, Hanover Square. The King and Queen had promised to be present. There was Royalty among my retinue of bridesmaids. I had received presents worth a small fortune."

"And then you ran away?" Gretna prompted, unable to wait for the end of the story.

"Yes, I ran away," Lady Rosemary replied. "I climbed down from my bedroom in the dead of night. Your father was waiting for me with a post-chaise at the gates and we galloped off to Gretna Green."

"And did Grandfather pursue you?"

"He did, indeed," her mother answered. "And nearly caught up with us, too. He had better horses and far more money to spend on the journey. Fortunately we had a whole night's start. They did not discover that I had gone until they went to call me in the morning."

"So you were married at Gretna Green."

"Yes, we were married at Gretna Green and your grandfather arrived half an hour later. He cursed me then, told me that I was no longer his daughter and whatever happened he never wished to see or hear of me again."

"Oh, Mamma! Did you mind?"

"I was upset at the time, but I had your father. That was all either of us wanted—to be together, to be allowed to love each other with all the affection and passion of which we were capable."

"And so you came here to live in the cottage?" Gretna said.

"At first we had no home and no money," Lady Rosemary replied. "People were very unkind to us as well because I had caused such a scandal. I had insulted the King and Queen, they said. I had made one of the most important noblemen in the country look a fool. I was assured—and I am quite certain they spoke the truth—that such a crime would never be forgiven me."

She put her hands to her eyes for a moment as if remembering all she had endured, before she went on:

"Then Mr. and Mrs. Walter Smythe took pity on us. They knew your father because he had once done Mr. Smythe some small service. They asked us to stay with them and later found us this cottage in the village so that we were near them. They have been Good Samaritans to us, Gretna, and we love them for it."

"And you have never regretted running away, Mamma?"

"Never, never! Not for one single instant," Lady Rosemary answered. There was no mistaking the sincerity in her tones. "If I could have even a shadow of regret, it would only be that I can never give you the chance of going to parties and balls, of coming out into Society, of meeting friends of your own age and in your own class."

"But, Mamma, I have friends here. There is Aunt Maria and dear Mrs. Merryweather at the farm."

Lady Rosemary had smiled but had not troubled to explain further. But as she had grown older still, Gretna had known what she meant. There was no-one in the tiny village with whom she could really be a playmate.

But there had always been "Aunt Maria". Gretna thought of her now and felt her heart quicken with excitement. The beautiful, exciting Maria Fitzherbert, whom she loved and who she knew loved her. At any moment now the carriage would be drawing up at her front door in Park Street.

She bent forward. Already the afternoon was drawing on. The stage-coach had been unconscionably slow doing the thirty miles to London, stopping at posting-inn after posting-inn and threading its way through the traffic of the metropolis at almost a snail's speed.

Gretna peered through the dirty windows of the hackney carriage. Yes, she could make out the words "Park Street" written on one of the tall, imposing houses past which they were driving. The street was long and it seemed to her, straight from the country, very impressive and magnificent.

The carriage came to a standstill. Gretna was ready to jump out long before the driver climbed down to open the door.

"Here is the money," she said, and the man took off his hat and thanked her. "Please put my luggage on the top step."

She ran up the steps and rang the bell. She could hear it clanging far away in the basement of the house. The cab-driver deposited her box beside her.

"Good day, lidy," he said, touching his hat; and climbing up on to the box of his coach, he whipped up his tired horse and drove away.

Gretna waited. She found herself shivering a little, not only because of the wind whistling down the street. It was chilly and the sun had disappeared behind some grey clouds, but colder still were her fears and anxieties. The conversation of the night before was fresh in her mind.

She realised that she had been waiting for quite a long time. Perhaps no-one had heard the bell, she thought, and rang again. This time there was the shuffle of heavy feet and then the clank of chains being removed. Finally the door opened slowly. An old, rheumaticky, bleary-eyed man stood there, a flickering candle in his hand, and beyond him Gretna could see an empty hall.

"Does not . . . Mistress Fitzherbert live . . . here?" she faltered.

"Gone away," was the answer, and the man made about to shut the door again.

"But, wait! Wait!" Gretna cried. "Where has she gone to?"

"Oi don't rightly know. Oi'm not th' caretaker. Me brother and his wife 'as the job, but they've 'ad to go to the country—'er ma's been taken bad. Oi'm only 'ere to 'elp out 'til they returns."

"But you must know where Mistress Fitzherbert is living now," Gretna said desperately. "If she has left the house, surely she would have left an address?"

"Oi don't rightly know. Me brother did say sum'at, but Oi can't recall what it was 'e said."

"Think, please think," Gretna begged.

"Ah, yes. Oi know. St. James's Square. That's where 'er 'as gone. St. James's Square."

The man shut the door with a bang, leaving Gretna staring rather helplessly at the brass knocker. This was something she had never anticipated for one moment. Then suddenly she realised with a sense of horror that Mistress Fitzherbert had never received her letter saying she was arriving. She had addressed the letter to this house in Park Street, but it was quite obvious that the man to whom she had just spoken would have been quite incapable of forwarding it on.

Somewhere in St. James's Square! What an impossible position for her to be in—to look for someone and not even know the number of the house. She would just have to ring any bell chosen at random and ask if they knew where Mistress Fitzherbert was likely to be residing.

The first thing was to find a hackney carriage. She went down the steps and stood on the edge of the pavement. Carriages were passing, but they none of them looked the type of vehicle which could be hired. There were big coaches with painted crests on their panels; there were smart curricles driven by supercilious grooms or smart young dandies with their beaver hats at an angle.

Gretna found herself staring at them, too interested at the moment to remember her own carriageless plight. Then suddenly a coach that had just driven past her was drawn up sharply a little further up the road. She hardly noticed it except to be aware that it was a private vehicle, until a voice beside her made her start.

"I thought it must be and now I am sure! Miss Gretna!"

She started round, her eyes wide, and saw Lord Wroxhall standing there, raising his hat with one hand and holding a gold-handled cane in the other. He was, in his elegance and his dark, leering eyes, the embodiment of everything she hated and everything she feared.

"Can I, perhaps be of assistance?" he asked.

"No, thank you, my Lord," Gretna said stiffly.

"You are waiting for someone?"

There was so much insinuation in his voice that she had to answer the truth.

"I am waiting for a hackney carriage."

"But why?" His smile revealed his white teeth which somehow resembled fangs. "My coach is here and I am at your service. Let me drive you where you wish to go."

"No, thank you, it is quite unnecessary. A hackney carriage will doubtless appear at any moment."

"And if it does, what an unpleasant, uncomfortable manner of travelling. Pray accept my hospitality. My coach is the very newest model and is almost—though I admit not quite—worthy of your beauty."

"I thank you, my Lord. I would rather find my own way to where I wish to go."

His eyes narrowed for a moment and he glanced up at the house behind her and at her box reposing on the top step.

"So you were visiting Mistress Fitzherbert?" he said. "How very strange!"

"I see nothing particularly strange in it," Gretna retorted.

"You were going to stay with her? You have, perhaps, an engagement in her household?"

"I thank your Lordship for your interest in me," Gretna said with all the dignity she could command. "But I would not wish to keep you standing here when you obviously have other commitments. I assure you that I am quite capable of hiring a carriage to carry me wherever I wish to go."

"What a long speech," he jeered. "And so proud, so independent. I wonder if you will be quite so imperious when you have been in London a little longer. You might even find me useful, who knows?"

Gretna made no answer but turned her head away, watching the road as the carriages passed in either direction.

"Does Stade know of this?" Lord Wroxhall asked from behind her bonnet. "Has he maybe concocted a little plot by which you are introduced into Mistress Fitzherbert's household, or am I mistaken?"

"I have nothing to say on this subject, my Lord," Gretna replied angrily.

"Somehow I think Stade does not know it," Lord Wroxhall said slowly, and Gretna knew that his eyes were scrutinising her, lingering on the plain, cheap gown she wore, on her simple shawl and untrimmed bonnet.

Last night he had suspected that the Marquis was her protector. Today he was not so sure. Her clothes contradicted any ideas he might have on that score.

She waved her hand suddenly. A hackney carriage was approaching, but as it drew nearer she saw it was occupied. She looked anxiously up the road and again anxiously down it. If only Lord Wroxhall would go away.

"Suppose, my dear, we have a little chat," he said. "Let me drive you to Mistress Fitzherbert's house in St. James's Square."

"Do you know it then? You know where she lives?"

Perhaps the question was over-anxious. At any rate he seized the advantage.

"I will take you there," he said. "I know the house and so does my coachman. 'Tis a waste of time waiting here for a hackney carriage which may never come."

"You are sure you know where she has gone?" Gretna asked, turning round to look at him.

"I promise you I do. Come, I swear I will not hurt you."

"I will come with you only on one condition, my Lord—that you do not touch me," Gretna said.

There was a smile on his lips and a light in his eyes as he bowed.

"You have my word on it."

With her head held high and with a dignity which might have been envied by any duchess, she walked slowly along the pavement towards his coach. He handed her into it and directed the footman to collect her box from the top of the steps. Then he got in beside her and the door was shut. There was a little delay and then the carriage started off.

"Now, tell me," Lord Wroxhall said, his voice soft and silky and, to Gretna, infinitely menacing, "why you are seeking Mistress Fitzherbert."

She was desperately afraid of him, but at least he was keeping his promise. She had squeezed herself as far into the corner of the coach as she could manage and he was sitting in the other corner and there was quite an appreciable distance of soft, cushioned seat between them.

"I have reasons of my own," she answered.

"How aloof you are to someone who only has your interests at heart."

She made no reply to this and after a moment he bent forward.

"Listen, my dear," he said. "Do not let us mince words between us. I can see that you are in poor circumstances. Let me be of assistance to you."

He saw her stiffen and added quickly:

"Not in the way you imagine, but in quite another manner."

"I do not know what you mean," Gretna said, merely because it seemed that she must say something.

"Let me tell you very plainly," Lord Wroxhall said. "I want information about Mistress Fitzherbert. If you are to stay in her house, it would be worth your while, well worth it, to see me occasionally, to relate to me any little details which might be of interest. Nothing sensational—do not be afraid of that—just your observation of ordinary, every-day occurrences."

"So you are asking me to be a spy?"

Gretna almost spat the words at him and had the satisfaction of seeing him look almost ashamed.

"Do you imagine that I would spy on anyone?" she went on. "Least of all on someone whom I respect and love. Yes, those are the right words, my Lord. I respect and love Mistress Fitzherbert and I can only imagine that you wish to spy on her because someone so good and decent as she would not allow a creature such as you even to cross the threshold of her house."

Gretna's scorn seemed to vibrate round the carriage. For a moment she thought she had nonplussed Lord Wroxhall and then she saw that he was chuckling.

"Magnificent!" he said. "Splendid! I had no idea you could look so beautiful. Aphrodite enraged! My dear, you enchant me."

"And I despise you," Gretna retorted.

He laughed again and then, to her relief, she realised the horses had come to a standstill and a footman was running down the steps of a house to open the door.

"We are here?" she asked.

"Let me assist you to alight," Lord Wroxhall said.

He stepped out of the coach first and Gretna prepared to follow him. Lord Wroxhall held his arm ready, pushing aside the footman with a muttered comment when he would have assisted her.

There was something in the man's face, some instinct that made her realise that the uniform he wore was the same as that of the footman on the box. Or perhaps it was just the guardianship of the angels over those who are endangered through innocence, but Gretna saw the open door ahead of her and turned accusingly.

"This is not Mistress Fitzherbert's house," she said. She glanced around. "And I will swear this is not St. James's Square."

"No, it is Berkeley Square, as it happens," Lord Wroxhall replied. "And I thought to offer you the hospitality of my house. I will not keep you long."

"You know full well I will not enter your house, my Lord," Gretna said.

She spoke in a low voice because even though she was angry she was ashamed to be seen brawling on the pavement in front of the servants.

"Come, do not be so prudish," Lord Wroxhall replied. "A glass of wine will do us both good."

He put his hand on her arm and in that split second she realised that unless she was careful he would take her by force. She was so small and he had only to link his arm firmly in hers and she would be helpless.

She eluded his hand and backed away from him.

"I must go, my Lord. Kindly instruct your footman to set down my box."

"Not so fast, my dear."

She saw by the look in his eyes that her very resistance excited him. He was determined now that he would take her where he wished and she knew, in that second, that she faced a danger greater than she had ever encountered before in the whole of her life.

Blindly she turned and ran from his outstretched hand, running along the pavement, not knowing where she was going, conscious, even as she ran, that he had started after her. There were people walking around who stared at her in amazement. And then, three or four doors higher up, a carpet was being run across the pavement by two footmen, while a third was opening the door of a black-and-gold cabriolet obviously built for speed.

Gretna was forced to pause for a moment to avoid the

flunkeys, and even as she did so a man stepped from the cabriolet. She was about to pass on. She had, in fact, already crossed the carpet and was on her toes ready to run even quicker than she had run before. Then she heard her own name.

"Gretna!"

She turned to look over her shoulder, her eyes wide with fear, her breath coming quickly between her lips. It was the Marquis who stood there, an expression of astonishment on his face.

"What in God's name are you doing?" he asked.

4

GRETNA STOOD STARING at the Marquis until he said coldly:

"I may be mistaken, but it appears to me that you are running away."

She felt the colour rise in her face as she looked back to where, further down the Square, Lord Wroxhall's coach stood outside his house. The servants, in their flamboyant livery, were moving to and from the coach. There was no sigh of its owner.

Gretna felt relief sweep over her. For a second she was too glad to be rid of Lord Wroxhall to remember that the Marquis was waiting for a reply to his question. Then she looked back at him and when at length she did speak the words came in a stammer:

"Y . . . yes . . . yes, I . . . I was running . . . away, my Lord."

"It appears to have become a habit," the Marquis said sarcastically.

Gretna blushed and dropped her head for a moment, and then remembered.

"My box!" she exclaimed. "It is on Lord Wroxhall's coach."

"I will send a servant for it," the Marquis said. "May I invite you to enter my house while he does so?"

"There is no need," Gretna said a little wildly. "All I require, my Lord, is a hackney carriage. I was endeavouring to find one when Lord Wroxhall insisted that he would convey me in his carriage to where I wished to go. And then . . ." The words came bursting out almost as if she felt the Marquis would not believe her and she was determined that he should listen to her explanation.

"I think," the Marquis interrupted suavely, "that what you have to reveal would be best said inside my house and not on the pavement."

It was rebuke and Gretna felt the colour deepen in her face.

"As your Lordship wishes," she agreed humbly. Then added quickly: "You will send for a hackney carriage?"

"A conveyance shall be provided for you," the Marquis replied.

There was nothing more that she could say, and meekly, feeling like a child who has been caught out in some misdemeanour, she walked through the door and into the cool quietness of a square hall. There was a flunkey to take the Marquis's cloak and hat, another to fling open the door of a long, low room where a fire burned brightly on the hearth and the tapers in crystal sconces revealed that the walls were lined with books.

Nervously Gretna moved across the room towards the fireplace, conscious that, although she had been running, the tips of her fingers were cold. As she did so, she knew that she was afraid—not of the Marquis himself, but of what he might think of her.

"I wish to give you an explanation, my Lord," she said as she reached the hearth and saw that he was standing a little way behind her, watching her with an expression on his face that she could not fathom.

He did not answer, and after a moment she went on:

"You must have thought it strangely ill-mannered of me to leave your house this morning without saying good-bye and without thanking you for your hospitality. I intended, of course, to write you a letter expressing my thanks."

"I shall await that letter with interest," the Marquis said.

Gretna looked down into the fire.

"I . . . I thought it best that Mrs. Merryweather and I should . . . leave the instant the stage-coach was ready."

"And yet I understand you had an hour's wait. Surely to be so precipitous was unnecessary?" the Marquis enquired.

As Gretna still stared into the fire and did not speak, he

came nearer and stood beside her, his eyes on her bent head.

"Why did you run away?" he asked, and his voice was low and deep.

"I . . . think I was . . . afraid, my Lord," she answered.

"Of what?" he insisted. "Lord Wroxhall had left. You had only your host to frighten you."

"Y ... you did not really ... frighten me," Gretna murmured. "And, yet . . . perhaps you . . . d . . . do. It was not really ... that, my Lord. It was ... m ... many things."

"I am sorry if I appear obtuse," the Marquis replied sarcastically, but there was a smile at the corner of his lips.

Gretna looked up at him.

"Please, my Lord, the hackney carriage should be here by now. May I go? I am anxious to find my friend."

"I gather she was not where you expected to find her."

Gretna shook her head.

"No, she has removed to another part of London, but I only discovered this after I had sent away the carriage that I had taken from the posting-stage. Lord Wroxhall saw me standing on the pavement and promised that he would drive me where I wished to go." Her voice ceased suddenly and then she said with something like a sob:

"H . . . he deceived me. He took me to his h . . . house. That . . . that was why I ran away."

"I see!"

The Marquis's tone was dry, and then when he spoke again his voice was kinder.

"Will you not be seated?" he asked. "I am going to send for wine and I shall insist on your drinking a glass because I think it will do you good. You have passed through an unpleasant experience."

He bent as he spoke and pulled at the embroidered bellrope. Almost immediately, as if he had been awaiting the summons, the door opened and a footman appeared.

"Wine and biscuits," the Marquis said briefly.

The footman vanished and as the door closed Gretna said: "I . . . I would rather go, my Lord."

"And I am determined you shall stay until you have drunk a glass of wine," he said with a smile. "Will you not sit down if I promise not to hurt you?"

She laughed at this a little tremulously and seated herself on the edge of a big damask-covered chair.

The Marquis said nothing and after a moment, as if his very silence eased the tension, Gretna undid the ribbons of her bonnet and pulling it off laid it on the floor beside her chair.

The firelight shone on her fair curls and they seemed as if they, too, were suddenly full of light and movement, as if glad to be released from the confines of the bonnet.

A moment later the wine and biscuits arrived and were set down on a small table.

"Leave them," the Marquis commanded, and when the footman had withdrawn he poured the wine from the decanter into a small, exquisitely cut crystal glass. He handed it to Gretna.

"Drink this," he said. "It will bring the colour back into your cheeks."

"I am not frightened any more," she protested.

"I am glad of that," he answered. "You still look rather like a child who has awoken from a nightmare."

Gretna shivered.

"I hate Lord Wroxhall," she said. "There is something about him, something in the way he speaks and looks, which makes me sure he is a bad man, an e . . . evil man."

"You must avoid him," the Marquis said. "He must not cross your path again."

"But supposing he does?" Gretna asked, her eyes dark at the thought of it.

"I have been thinking about that," the Marquis said slowly. "In fact, I was thinking of you as I travelled to London this afternoon."

"Of me?" Gretna asked.

"Does that surprise you?" he asked.

She dropped her eyes before the look in his.

"I expected you to be in . . . incensed with me, my Lord," she said. "I have been rude, ungrateful, but in the night it seemed the right thing to do."

"The thoughts we think at night are usually distorted," the Marquis answered. "I have been thinking of you in the daytime, and to be frank I am perturbed as to what will happen to you in London."

"It is kind of your Lordship, but there is no reason for anyone to worry about me," Gretna said quickly. "When I find my friend, she will look after me."

"I hope she is capable of it," the Marquis remarked coldly as if it was improbable that she would be.

Gretna was just about to protest when she remembered

what he thought of Mistress Fitzherbert and pressed her lips together.

"I must get away," she thought to herself a little wildly. She picked up her bonnet from the floor and rose to her feet.

"I would not appear rude for the second time, my Lord," she said. "But 'tis getting late. I have to find my friend and I wish to be on my way."

"My carriage is waiting for you and will convey you wherever you desire to go," he replied.

"Your carriage!" she exclaimed in dismay. "Oh, I would not want to put you to any inconvenience. A hackney carriage is all I require."

"Since you have not been particularly fortunate in that mode of transport up till now, I suggest you avail yourself of my offer," the Marquis retorted. "My coachman is entirely trustworthy, and if it will make you any happier I will not offer to accompany you."

"I thank you, my Lord," Gretna said in such a tone of relief that he laughed.

"You are at least honest," he said. "Is my company really so obnoxious to you?"

"No, no, please, you are not to think that," Gretna said quickly. She wrung her hands. "Oh, dear! Once again I am being rude. I did not mean it, my Lord, I promise you."

"I believe you," he said. "I can quite understand your feelings in not wishing to arrive at your friend's house with a gentleman in attendance. It would only require more explanations. No, you must just tell her that after an accident to the stage-coach, which happened near my house, I arranged for my coach to see you safely to your destination's end. Will that suffice?"

"Yes indeed."

"Well, that is settled then."

"I had best go," Gretna said, making a move as if to walk towards the door.

"One moment!"

The Marquis's voice arrested her. She had half turned away from him. Now she turned back. He was looking very grave, she thought, and yet somehow she fancied there was still a ghost of a smile at the corner of his mouth.

She could not help thinking how well he fitted into this luxurious, and yet so obviously a man's room. His travelling coat of steel grey was plain enough; and yet anything he wore appeared to acquire an elegance and, at the same time, a grandeur which Gretna thought suddenly would have made him outstanding in whatever company he found himself.

She realised suddenly that after commanding her to wait he had not spoken, and now she looked up wonderingly into his face, curious as to what he was about to say.

Slowly, as if he deliberated over his words, he set the glass of wine he held in his hand, and which he had left almost untouched, down on the polished table, before he said:

"I told you that I had been thinking about you as I travelled towards London. I had not thought to see you so soon, but had planned to find out your address by sending one of my servants to enquire at the farm of your aunt, Mrs. Merryweather."

"Oh, but you must not do that," Gretna said quickly.

"Why not?" he enquired.

"Well, there is no need," Gretna answered. "I am here. You have found me. It would be quite unnecessary, would it not, for you to make enquiries now that we have met?"

"Quite, I agree," the Marquis said. "I am only informing you what I intended to do."

"It was kind of you to be interested." Gretna murmured.

"It would be more to the point," he answered, "to ask why I was so anxious to see you."

"Yes, of course," Gretna agreed, and then hesitated, at a loss for words.

"It was because I had a wish to see you again," the Marquis explained. "And because, too, I was perturbed as to what would happen to you in London. You see, my dear, you are very lovely, and London is not at all the place for lovely young women to be on their own, or with only another woman for protection."

"I . . . I suppose not," Gretna said in a small voice.

"And, therefore, when I had found you," the Marquis went on. "I was going to suggest that you might care to look on me as—your protector."

There was a moment's silence and then Gretna said in a bewildered voice:

"But . . . I do not . . . understand."

"I think you do," the Marquis answered. "You are young and quite obviously innocent. At the same time, you are old enough to know what Lord Wroxhall wants of you."

The blood came flooding into Gretna's small face.

"You . . . mean . . ." she faltered, and then her voice died away in her throat.

"Exactly," the Marquis said drily. "And although I am hoping that it might seem to you better than just the best of two evils, I am offering to look after you myself."

"But . . . but how?" Gretna stammered.

"The details can be thought out later when we have come to some agreement," the Marquis said with a smile. "Perhaps a house in Chelsea, a carriage of your own, or anything else you might fancy. Sufficient to say that no-one will insult you when it is known that if they do they must answer to me."

"A house in Chelsea and a carriage!" Gretna repeated, and then suddenly the full impact of what the Marquis was saying dawned upon her bewildered brain.

"No! No!" she said sharply. "No, of course not!"

She turned away from him as she spoke and stood holding on to a nearby chair as if for support. It could not be true, she thought. He could not be suggesting such a thing to her. What would her mother have said?

"Is it because we have not known each other very long that this has come as a surprise to you?" the Marquis asked. "Or is perhaps your little head full of romantic notions and you do not think that you are in love?"

He smiled that strange, cynical smile of his and then, drawing nearer to her, almost before she was aware of it, put out his hand gently and touched the smooth roundness of her neck. Just for a moment he seemed to clasp it as a man might clasp the soft feathers of a bird that was anxious to fly away from him, and then his fingers moved upwards and cupped her chin, to turn her face up to his.

"Shall I make you fall in love with me?" he asked in his deep voice.

Her eyes were held by his. For a moment she could think of nothing and see nothing save the dark depths behind which it seemed to her she saw a flicker of fire.

Then before she could move, before she could realise what was happening, his lips were on hers. She felt him take her in his arms and it seemed as if the whole world vanished and she herself ceased to exist. She no longer had any entity or will-power, she was no longer a person but a part of him.

She felt as if his kiss took not only her mouth but her whole body into his keeping. She felt as if he suddenly dived with her from a high cliff into the deep green waters of the ocean and that they went down, down together into a bottomless world from which they might never return.

How long he held her captive she had no idea. She only knew that as he released her she was trembling all over and yet hardly conscious of what her thoughts or feelings were.

"Would it be very hard to love me, little Gretna?" he asked, and there was a note of triumph in his voice as if he was a conqueror aware of how complete was his conquest.

In answer Gretna put her fingers up to her lips as if to make sure her mouth was still there after he had taken possession of it.

"No! No!" she cried, but her voice was stifled in her throat. "You do not . . . understand. Please . . . please . . . let me . . . go."

She would have run from him, but his hands were on her shoulders.

"Tell me what troubles you and I will try to understand," he said. "You must learn to trust me. Then I promise you we shall deal very well together."

"I must . . . go! I . . . I must go!" Gretna pleaded. There was such desperation in her voice that his hands fell from her shoulders and she saw there was a look almost of disappointment on his face.

"Very well," he said. "Go now and we will talk of this matter later. There is no hurry, except for my own anxiety to have things settled. May I call on you tomorrow?"

"No! Yes. I . . . I do not kn . . . know," Gretna stammered.

He laughed gently at that and taking her hand raised her quivering fingers to his lips.

"Do not keep me waiting too long before you give me an answer," he said.

He escorted her without further words to the front door. The footman ran to lay down the carpet across the pavement and to open the coach door with its emblazoned crest and silver handles.

"Tomorrow," the Marquis said softly, and then Gretna was in the coach and he had turned back towards the house.

"Where to, Miss?" the footman asked as he arranged a fur rug over Gretna's knees.

Gretna looked over his shoulder. She could see that by now the Marquis had reached the front door and was stepping into the hall.

"Drive towards St. James's Square," she said quietly, "but before you reach there stop at a rank where hackney carriages wait. I wish to be set down and to hire one."

"Very good, Miss."

The footman did not even look surprised. He had been well trained not to question the orders of the aristocracy, however fantastic their requests might be.

He shut the door and the coach set off. Gretna lay back against the soft cushions and covered her face with her hands. What was happening to her? What had she been doing? How could she have permitted the Marquis to kiss her and to have made no protest? And, what was more, he had offered her his protection.

She understood at last what he had meant, and knew that she should be ready to die of shame. And yet she could blame no-one but herself. When Mrs. Merryweather had made the preposterous assertion that she was her niece, she should either have contradicted her then or explained later to the Marquis when they arrived at Stade Hall.

Everything would then have been different. He would not have expected her to dine alone with him. She would not have been found by Lord Wroxhall. She would not have laid herself open to the insults of both noblemen such as she had endured in the last hour.

What a tangle it all was! And yet she had no-one to blame but herself. One thing was quite certain—she must never, under any circumstances, meet either Lord Wroxhall or the Marquis again.

That should be easy, she thought. For when she was once with her dear Aunt Maria, everything would smooth itself out and there would be no need for any further fears. Just for a moment she wondered if there could be any truth in Lord Wroxhall's tales and if the Prince was really enamoured of Aunt Maria. Then she dismissed the whole thing as quite ridiculous and absurd.

No-one could live more simply or like a quiet existence more than Maria Fitzherbert. Why, Gretna had even heard her say once, when they talked of London: "The London I know is very different from the London one hears about by rumour or reads about in books. I live a very secluded existence with only a few dear and close friends to keep me company."

That had been two years ago and Mr. Fitzherbert had been dead for three years. There was no reason to think that his widow would have changed her style of living, especially not to the extent that Lord Wroxhall had suggested.

"It is one of his wicked lies," Gretna said aloud.

She realised that the coach was pulling up beside the pavement. They were in a broad, busy street and she guessed, though she had never been there before, that it was Piccadilly. She could see the footman running across the road and speaking to the driver of a rather dilapidated vehicle drawn by a thin, unkempt horse.

The coach door was opened and Gretna stepped out; her box was transferred to the hackney carriage and she gave the footman one of her last shillings.

"Thank you very much," she said.

"Where shall I tell him to drive to, Miss?" the footman enquired.

"St. James's Square," Gretna said. "I will instruct him further when we get there."

"Very good, Miss."

The footman shut the door and the hackney carriage set off slowly.

The seat on which Gretna was sitting felt hard and cold after the soft luxury of the Marquis's coach. They drove for only a short distance before the carriage pulled up. Gretna opened the window and put out her head.

"Is this St. James's Square?" she asked.

"That's right, Missie. They didn't give me no other address."

"I am afraid I do not know the house," Gretna said. "But if you wait a moment I will enquire of a passer-by. Someone may have knowledge of where the lady I am seeking resides."

"Well, Missie, I knows that the Earl of Landsale lives 'ere," the coach-driver said, pointing with his whip to the nearest house. "And His Grace of Severn next door. I knows 'im well enough. Mean as a miser 'e be. Won't use 'is own coach for fear it should cost 'im anything, and never parts with a penny piece for those as drives 'im."

"Perhaps, as you know so many of the houses," Gretna

ventured, "you know where Mistress Fitzherbert's residence is."

" 'Er! Oh, I knows where 'er lives right enough. Who don't?" the coachman said. "And if you didn't know, you'd only have to follow 'is Royal 'ighness 'ere from Carlton 'ouse Terrace. That'd tell ye." He started to laugh at his own joke and then fell to coughing.

"Perhaps you will be kind enough to drive me there," Gretna said with what dignity she could command.

She shut the coach window with a little bang. As she sat down on the seat again her eyes were wide with dismay. It couldn't be true! It couldn't! There must be some mistake. That Aunt Maria should be spoken of in such a manner. She who had always been so quiet and so fastidious.

Gretna tried to reconcile the stories she had heard with her own faith and trust in the woman she had loved ever since she was a baby.

The Prince of Wales might love Aunt Maria—that was understandable enough, although it was difficult to think how she could have met him, living as quielty as she did. But even if he loved her, there would have been no excuse for such rumours to have got about such as Lord Wroxhall had repeated. It would be impossible for Aunt Maria to marry him, and never, never would she stoop to occupying any other position. Gretna was sure of that.

As she thought of it, her chin went up, as if her own pride and honour were at stake. Aunt Maria would never live under the protection of any man—not even if he were heir to the Crown of England. She was so convinced of this that she was smiling again as the carriage stopped and she alighted.

The house at which they had stopped surprised her. It was large—one of the largest houses in the Square—and it was with some trepidation that Gretna walked up the stone steps to raise the brightly burnished silver knocker.

The door was opened immediately. A footman stood there and Gretna knew at once that she had come to the right place. He was wearing livery that she had seen so often when Maria Fitzherbert had visited her parents at Brambridge—green and gold with silver buttons. It was quite familiar, but she had never before seen Maria Fitzherbert's servants in white silk stockings and powdered wigs.

"I wish to see Mistress Fitzherbert," Gretna said in a low voice.

"Madam is not receiving this afternoon," the flunkey replied in what seemed to Gretna a very aloof, almost insolent manner.

"Even so, I am sure she will see me," Gretna insisted. "Please to tell her Miss Gretna Hayden is here."

"Madam is not receiving," the footman insisted. "If you will call tomorrow, she may be able to see you then."

He made as if to shut the door. Gretna was not to be intimidated.

"Kindly tell Mistress Fitzherbert that her niece is here," she commanded.

The footman instantly unbent.

"I am sorry, Miss. I did not know you were a relation. Madam had not said you were expected. Will you be pleased to enter?"

"My box is in the carriage and please pay the coachman his due," Gretna said, and moved into a hall which seemed even more luxurious and impressive than the Marquis's had been.

The footman opened a pair of high mahogany doors.

"If you will wait here a moment, Miss, I will inform Madam of your arrival."

Gretna found herself in a square room, exquisitely furnished, which seemed to her characteristic of Maria Fitzherbert. There were flowers and soft cushions; there was an embroidery frame with quite a lot of the design completed; there were also two books lying open as if the reader had just laid them down.

What was more, there were several little water-colour sketches of Brambridge, all signed with the initials "M.S.". They were done, as Gretna well knew, when Maria was first in her teens. She had loved sketching and often Gretna had gone with her to tumble and play about in the hay while Maria sketched the house, the water-lily pond or the distant view through the great trees in the park.

Gretna felt her heart leap with excitement. She had arrived. This was journey's end; and although it had taken her through many difficulties and obstacles to reach here, it was silly of her to have been so frightened. Now all she had endured seemed trivial beyond the fact that she was here—very trivial except for one thing.

Her thin fingers went to her lips. She could still feel the warm strength of the Marquis's mouth and she knew then that she had been trying not to think of his kiss, not to remember that strange, unaccountable weakness in herself.

She had fought against recalling it from the moment she had left his house in Berkeley Square until this moment, and yet now it came flooding back to her—the touch of his fingers on her throat, the manner in which he had turned her face up to his, and then his lips, strong, possessive and yet unaccountably tender. She had not known a man's mouth could be so soft.

"It should never have happened," Gretna whispered, and yet she knew that because it had happened she would never be able to forget it.

She felt herself tremble again, felt that same strange, unaccountable weakness seep over her so that her knees felt that they could no longer hold her. She would have fallen when he kissed her had not his arms held her so tightly, she thought. She was ready to fall now at the very memory of it.

She tried to think of something else. She moved across the room, stared at the pictures on the wall and the water-colours of Brambridge. She couldn't see the long, low, comfortable house. Instead she saw two dark eyes looking down into hers and heard a voice say: "Would it be very hard to love me, little Gretna?"

She turned eagerly as the door opened. Here at last was an interruption to her memories. The footman stood there.

"Madam asks if you will come upstairs, Miss," he announced.

Gretna followed him up the wide, carved staircase to polished doors which she was sure were the entrance to the Salon. She was not mistaken. The footman threw them open.

"Miss Gretna Hayden, Madam," he announced.

Gretna had a confused impression of lights and colours; and then she saw Maria Fitzherbert, lovelier than even she had remembered her, her pale gold hair in curls all over her head, her eyes alight with pleasure, her hands outstretched.

"Gretna! Gretna! My darling!" she exclaimed as she ran towards her.

Gretna found herself clasped in loving arms; there was a soft cheek against hers, a voice asking a dozen eager questions.

Then over Maria Fitzherbert's shoulder she saw, leaning

against the mantelpiece, the handsome face and elegant figure of a young man whom, even if she had not seen his picture, she would have known to be the Prince of Wales.

5

"I AM so deeply distressed, dearest Gretna, that I never received your letter," Maria Fitzherbert said for the tenth time as Gretna somewhat stumblingly related how she had arrived in London to find a very poor reception at the deserted house in Park Street.

"All the same," she continued, "your letter should undoubtedly have been brought here to me. I will send a footman to Park Street immediately to find out what is happening. The caretaker must be told to let me know if there is illness and he cannot carry out his duties."

"It was tiresome of me to arrive at such short notice," Gretna said apologetically. "But I had no idea what else to do."

"You were quite right to come," Maria Fitzherbert assured her. "Indeed, have I not often said over and over again that I was always there if you needed me?"

"All the same, I feel embarrassed at forcing myself upon you," Gretna said. "But Mrs. Merryweather was determined that it was the right thing for me to do."

"Dear Mrs. Merry! How is she? In good health I trust?" Maria Fitzherbert asked.

Gretna looked embarrassed. She had not yet related what had happened on the journey or how she and Mrs. Merryweather had spent the night at Stade Hall. She had thought it would be easy to tell her dear Aunt Maria everything, but with the Prince of Wales sitting and listening to every word she felt it was impossible to relate what had happened, especially as regards the Marquis and Lord Wroxhall.

"What is more important than your enquiries about this Mrs. Merryweather," the Prince said now, "is to decide how we shall launch the beautiful Miss Hayden upon the *beau monde*."

He was teasing her, Gretna thought, and yet he smiled

so charmingly as he spoke and she felt that anything he said could not but sound pleasant.

There was no doubt at all that he was a very attractive young man. He was tall with broad shoulders and his elegance and exquisite manners were almost overwhelming to Gretna.

The Prince was dressed with great richness and she remembered, as she looked at his embroidered waistcoat with its jewelled buttons and the exquisite texture of his coat with its high velvet collar, that someone had once said that he spent over ten thousand pounds a year on clothes.

But she was not prepared to criticise him whatever he did, for from the moment of her arrival he had gone out of his way to make her feel at ease. Indeed, she was soon smiling at him and finding him as easy to talk to as if he had been just an ordinary gentleman.

The clock on the mantelpiece struck the hour and Maria gave an exclamation.

"You must go, Sire," she said. "You know you have an appointment with Sir James Harris."

"He can wait," the Prince of Wales said easily.

Maria shook her head.

"No, you must leave," she insisted. "I would not wish Sir James to think that I detained you when he may have matters of import to discuss. You will remember that he has been with His Majesty all day."

"Then anything he has to tell me must certainly be disagreeable," the Prince replied almost petulantly, but Gretna noticed that in obedience to Maria's wishes he rose to his feet.

"I shall see you this evening at Carlton House?" he asked almost anxiously, as if it was hard for him to tear himself away even for a few hours.

"I shall be there, Sire," Maria Fitzherbert replied reassuringly.

"And you will bring your little guest with you?" the Prince enquired with a gesture towards Gretna.

Maria Fitzherbert shook her head.

"Not tonight, Sire. If she is to blossom out, as you suggested, and make an impression on Society, she must have some beautiful gowns. They take time to choose and to make."

"Yes, of course," the Prince said. "Well, I am quite certain I can leave all such details in your very capable hands, Maria. But I shall be delighted to sponsor her début."

"That is indeed kind of you, Sire," Maria smiled, with a glance at Gretna which made her drop down in a deep curtsy.

"I . . . I thank your . . . Royal Highness," she stammered.

The Prince kissed Maria's hand, bowed to Gretna and then went from the room, moving with a grace which did not in any way detract from his masculinity.

As the door closed behind him, Maria gave a sigh.

"Isn't he kind?" she asked Gretna. "You see, he thinks of everyone. And now that he has promised to sponsor your début you are made, dearest, as far as Society is concerned."

"I know, Aunt Maria, I——" Gretna began, only to be interrupted.

"Oh, my love!" Maria exclaimed. "I beg of you not to call me Aunt. I know you have done so from your childhood, but it makes me seem so old, so very old; and, as you know, I did, in fact, but reach twenty-nine years on my last birthday."

"No, I understand," Gretna said. "But what shall I call you?"

"Just Maria. Really, in appearance, we might almost be sisters, only you, in fact, would be a very little sister compared with me with my height."

They both laughed, but it was true. There was a resemblance in their colouring. But while Maria Fitzherbert, for all her prettiness, had a pronounced aquiline nose, Gretna's tiny little tip-tilted nose was very different. And she was much smaller. In height she barely reached to the older woman's chin—and her eyes seemed almost too big for the small oval of her face.

But they both had abundant hair of pale gold, which Maria, in defiance of the fashion, wore unpowdered, their complexions were like wild roses and their figures full of grace.

But while they did not realise it, they actually resembled each other more in other ways—in their vivacity, their good nature and their unaffected manners, which in both rose from a kindness of heart and an unfailing love of people and of life itself.

"And now, dearest, we have so many things to talk about," Maria said, drawing Gretna down on the sofa beside her. "First let me look at you. I hardly recognise my little girl—you have grown so pretty."

"You always were lovely," Gretna answered, "but somehow you too have altered."

"In what way?" Maria asked.

"You seem gayer and . . . much more elegant," Gretna replied. "You appear to me—although, of course I am very ignorant—to be dressed in the height of fashion; and that somehow is unlike you."

Maria rose from the sofa and walked to the fireplace. For a moment she had her back to Gretna, but the mirror reflected that her eyes were troubled and the smile was missing from her red lips. Gretna waited apprehensively. She wondered if what she had said was wrong. Then Maria turned.

"Gretna," she said, "I have loved you ever since you were a baby and I think you have loved me."

"You know I have," Gretna answered. "I have loved you always—more than anyone else in the world, except for Papa and Mamma."

"Then there is something I want to say to you," Maria went on. "You have come here to London. I want you to live with me. But I want first to know that you love me enough to trust me."

She moved suddenly and knelt down beside Gretna as she sat on the sofa, her full-skirted dress of white satin billowing around her, the soft fichu round her shoulders and her breasts moving a little convulsively as if with the intensity of her feelings.

"Listen to me, Gretna," she said. "You are going to find London a very difficult place in which to live. You will hear things said that will shock and surprise you. People are only happy when they are repeating unkind gossip or taking away someone's character. They will talk of me; they may even tell you many wicked and cruel things about me."

"I should not believe them," Gretna said.

"You may find it very hard to refute them," Maria said, and her eyes were full of pain. "But because we love each other, because you have known me for so long, will you promise to trust me?"

"But of course," Gretna answered.

"No, do not say it like that," Maria interrupted. "I do not want you to make a promise you cannot keep. But I want you to be sure in your heart that I would never do anything that was wrong, anything that would hurt my soul or my hope of everlasting life."

"I know you would never do anything like that," Gretna cried.

"It will not be easy for you," Maria went on, almost as if she had not heard. "I ought really to send you somewhere else, but I am selfish enough to want you to stay here with me. It will be so lovely to have a friend, someone who believes in me, someone whom I, too, can trust."

"Oh, let me stay, dearest Maria, let me stay," Gretna begged. "I could not bear to go elsewhere when I want so much to be with you."

"We will not speak of this again," Maria answered. "But you will remember that I have asked you to trust me and to do so with your heart and not your mind."

"I will remember," Gretna promised, and it was almost in the nature of a vow.

Maria put her arms around her and kissed her; and then, still linked together, they walked up the stairs to the bedrooms.

Gretna's box containing the few meagre things she had brought with her had already been unpacked and the fire was lit in a pretty little room overlooking the Square. There was a small four-poster draped with muslin curtains and a dressing-table with muslin petticoats round it to match. It was all very fresh and gay and made Gretna think of the gardens of the Fitzherberts' home at Brambridge.

"I hope you will be happy in this room," Maria said as she looked around her to see everything was in place.

"I have just been thinking as we came upstairs," Gretna said. "Did His Royal Highness realise, when he was so kind, who I am?"

"Who you are, dearest! What do you mean?"

"I mean . . . did he know that Mamma ran away with Papa? I did not like to say anything, but perhaps when he realises what happened he will withdraw his kind invitation to Carlton House and feel that perhaps it would be best for me not to go out into Society."

"Whatever put such a nonsensical idea into your funny little head?" Maria asked.

"But do you not understand?" Gretna said. "Mamma has said so often how by running away on the very eve of her marriage she insulted the King and Queen and held the Duke of Avon—who, after all, was of vast consequence—up to ridicule."

"A very good thing too, if you ask me," Maria laughed. "He is a pompous, disagreeable old man, and although perhaps your mother was to blame, he is certainly soured with life and takes care that everyone shall know it."

"But Their Majesties?"

Maria gave a little laugh.

"Dearest, I do not intend to try and initiate you in a few seconds into all the emotional tangles you will find at Court. But I can assure you that the Prince is a law unto himself and if the King takes up one attitude he is almost certain to take the other."

"They do not get on well together?" Gretna asked.

"Very badly I am afraid," Maria replied sadly. "I do my best, but it is not easy for me, for I, in particular, am a bone of contention."

"The Prince loves you very much, doesn't he?" Gretna asked.

"He is a very wonderful person," Maria answered with a catch in her voice. "And I love him, Gretna! It may be a mistake, but I love him with all my heart. It is impossible for me to deny it."

There was so much suffering in her tone that Gretna instinctively put her arms around her.

"Oh, Maria, how hard it must be for you! But he loves you too."

"Yes, he loves me," Maria said softly. "Loves me more than anyone knows or imagines. He loves me enough to make sacrifices for my sake that are almost unbelievable."

She was silent for a moment and then, as if she thrust some hidden thought away from her, she said in a very different tone:

"I must go and dress for the party tonight. Why do you not change your travelling gown and then come and talk to me? I should like that above all things."

"But of course I will," Gretna agreed.

"I will send a maid to you," Maria said. "You will find my bedroom a little way down the passage at the top of the stairs. Do not hurry yourself unduly. My hairdresser always takes an unconscionable time."

"Your hair is so pretty!" Gretna exclaimed. "But you are doing it in a new fashion."

"Yes, and we must see if yours can be done the same

way," Maria answered. "It is called *à la hedgehog;* it is amusing."

"It is very becoming," Gretna said in admiration, and Maria bent to kiss her cheek before she hurried from the room, leaving a faint fragrance of expensive perfume behind her.

Gretna had no time, for the next few hours, to think of the Marquis or what he must think of her second hurried departure. It was only when finally Maria Fitzherbert had left for Carlton House, carrying a fan glittering with brilliants and looking so beautiful in a huge looped gown of pale blue brocade with a diamond necklace that Gretna could only stare at her as if she was a being from another world, that at last she could consider her own reactions.

The house seemed empty without her. It was as if it was suddenly hushed, although the echo of Maria's laughter and her gay voice seemed somehow to whisper in the silence.

Gretna went slowly up the stairs. She had said that she would prefer to have a bowl of soup and perhaps a dish of chicken on a tray in her bedroom. She was afraid of the formality she might find in the dining-room.

She had never expected that Maria would have a whole army of butlers and footmen, housekeepers and maids to attend her wishes. And now Gretna realised that she would have to readjust her whole idea of the life that they were to live together. Indeed, she must alter her ideas on many things, for while she was dressing Maria had said to her:

"Do not worry what people will think of your mother's escapade all those years ago. Why, I assure you, it will add considerably to the interest you will arouse."

"Will they not be shocked?" Gretna asked.

Maria had laughed that free, untrammelled laugh which seemed to ring out like the tinkle of silver bells.

"But of course not, you stupid child. They will only think it romantic and exciting—as, indeed, it must have been. I always envied your mother so much that wild adventure, especially because it brought her such unadulterated happiness."

"So much happiness," Gretna said slowly, "that without Papa she did not wish to go on living. They had always been so close to each other, so utterly happy together."

"I shall never forgive myself for not knowing what was happening," Maria sighed. "But I was abroad and the letter relating your father's death never reached me. I moved from place to place rather quickly and left no address behind. There were . . . reasons for my doing that."

The maid was in the room and Gretna realised that it would be embarrassing to ask what the reasons might be. But somehow, instinctively, she guessed that they concerned the Prince. She could not help remembering that Lord Wroxhall, in that conversation with the Marquis which she had overheard, had said that Maria had been abroad until December. It was after she returned that it was rumoured that she had married the Prince.

That was, of course, impossible, as Gretna well knew. And yet if Maria was not married to the Prince, what then was their relationship? Alone in her bedroom, she felt her face burn at the thought. And then, resolutely, she refused to think of it. Maria had asked her to trust her. That she was prepared to do and any questions or even thoughts on the matter were treasonable.

She had her supper in front of the fire and then walked to the writing-table. It was only a small piece of furniture, French in design with exquisitely inlaid panels, but there was engraved writing-paper in the pigeon-holes and a new quill pen standing up like a sentinel in a shining silver ink-pot.

First Gretna wrote a letter to Mrs. Merryweather telling her that she had arrived safely and that Maria was in good health. She thanked her for escorting her to London and asked her to write soon and say if her health and bruises were better.

Then she hesitated for a long time. Night had fallen outside the window, but she stared out into the darkness of the Square. She was remembering a deep voice with just a hint of amusement in it saying: "Shall I make you fall in love with me?" And she was recalling that stupefying moment when she had felt the Marquis's arms around her and his mouth had captured hers.

She felt herself quiver and tremble as she felt again the strange sensation that had swept over her, the weakness which had made her unable to move or cry out and which had left her helpless in his arms.

"How dared he?" she whispered aloud, and yet there was no anger in her voice, only an astonishment and surprise that she had not felt more incensed at the time.

"I must never see him again," she told herself, and then

wondered what would happen if they met at Carlton House. There would be so many people there, she told herself quickly, that it would be easy to avoid him. Anyway, he would not dream for a moment that the well-dressed Miss Hayden, whose début was sponsored by the Prince of Wales himself, could possibly be the same as the badly dressed niece of fat Mrs. Merryweather to whom he had offered his protection.

Why should he connect the two? And who, indeed, would dare insult the social Miss Hayden with such a suggestion as the Marquis had made to simple Miss Gretna from the farm?

Yet somehow Gretna could not be angry with him on that score. In a way he had been trying to do her a kindness, to rescue her from the attentions of Lord Wroxhall, to protect her from the evils and menaces of a city of which she knew so little.

She took up a piece of writing-paper and with the ivory paper-knife cut off the address from the top of it. Then slowly, in her delicate handwriting, she wrote:

My Lord,

This is to thank Your Lordship for your Hospitality and to assure You that I have reached my Friend in Safety. We shall never meet again, but once again I thank You most sincerely for your Kindness.

Gretna.

She read it through several times, assured herself that she could not improve upon it; then slipping it into an envelope, she addressed it to the Marquis in Berkeley Square.

When the maid came in to make up the fire and turn down her bed, Gretna gave her the note.

"Will you have this posted?" she asked.

"It would be quite easy for one of the footmen to take it, Miss."

"No, no," Gretna protested. "I want it franked and sent through the post. Will you make that clearly understood downstairs?"

"It shall be as you say. Miss," the maid answered.

She went from the room, but not before Gretna had an impulse to take the letter back. Perhaps it was better to say nothing, and yet she had been brought up not only to have good manners, but also to be grateful. She could not bring herself to ignore the Marquis altogether even though, as she had said in the letter, they would never meet again.

She felt unaccountably depressed at the thought and told herself that there had been something exhilarating besides frightening about him. Then she remembered again how he had kissed her, and thought that no-one, not even Maria, must ever know what had occurred.

She slipped into bed. She had thought she was tired after the journey, the early rising and the emotions of the night before, but instead of sleeping she lay awake for a very long time. Some time later still, when the dawn was beginning to lighten the sky above the rooftops, she thought she heard a coach outside. Through her dreams she thought, too, she heard a voice—a man's voice—in the house. But she was not sure of it and at last she fell into a deep and dreamless slumber from which she did not awake until nearly noon.

The next days were spent almost entirely in standing while gowns were fitted on her. She must turn first this way and then that to be certain that the hem was the right length, that the bodice fitted, the waist was not too tight.

At first she was entranced with the satins, the brocades, the muslins, which were hung upon her, each one seeming more alluring than the last. Then she began to get rather bored with it all.

There were not only gowns, there were hats and bonnets of many different shapes trimmed with flowers and feathers and made of chipstraw or silk edged with lace. There were shoes to be fitted, there were silk stockings to be bought and petticoats, chemises and shifts to be ordered from a Convent where the Nuns embroidered them as if with fairy fingers.

"You are too kind and generous to me," Gretna cried over and over again.

But Maria only laughed and ordered more.

When, three days after her arrival, Gretna was told that she was to go to Carlton House that evening, she felt as if the curtains were being drawn back on a dramatic and exciting play in which she had the rôle of the heroine.

Everything she had done since she arrived at St. James's Square appeared to have been in the light of a rehearsal for just this moment. Maria had taught her to curtsy in the correct Court manner; she had shown her how to wield her fan in what was considered the most enticing and elegant way; she had shown her which knives and forks were used for the long, elaborate dinner-parties which apparently the Prince enjoyed every night of his life.

"I tell him he is a *gourmet*," Maria said with a little laugh, "but he says that he only wants the best of everything in life, and when one thinks of his miserable childhood one can understand why."

"Was he really miserable?" Gretna enquired.

Maria looked over her shoulder as if to be certain that no-one was listening.

"The King was so jealous of him," she said in a low voice, "that the Prince passed his boyhood shut up in a Palace that was almost a prison, deprived of all ordinary amusements. His father insisted on treating him as a child when he was a boy and as a boy when he was a man. It was not until he was nineteen, when he legally came of age as heir to the Throne, that the King could no longer keep him under lock and key and was compelled to grant him a small establishment of his own."

"Why was the King so unkind?" Gretna asked.

Maria shrugged her shoulders.

"No-one knows," she replied. "But His Majesty is a very strange man. Sometimes people wonder if he is entirely sane, but do not say I said so. I must not criticise, but sometimes I burn with indignation when I see what His Royal Highness has to suffer."

It was obvious that the Prince brought all his sufferings, whatever they might be, to Maria. Every day he came to the house at times which were arranged and at which Maria was expecting him. Every night they dined together.

Gretna learnt that the Prince would accept no invitations to a private house unless Maria was also invited. Some of the great London hostesses were annoyed by this, but they could not afford to offend the Prince and so invitations for Maria flooded into the house in St. James's Square.

Gretna wondered if sometimes these big formal parties were not more of a pain than a pleasure to Maria.

"I would want to be alone with the man I loved," she told herself, "instead of having to watch him surrounded by fawning Courtiers and beautiful women who flatter him and try their best to entice away his affection."

But there were other occasions when the Prince would arrive unheralded and unexpected in St. James's Square. He would burst into the room where Maria and Gretna were seated together.

"What do you think he has done now, Maria?" he would ask, and there was no doubt at all of whom he was speaking.

And Gretna, after curtsying deeply, would withdraw, leaving them together, knowing that by the time the Prince had been with Maria for half an hour or so the anger would have gone from his blue eyes and his irresistible smile would be curving his lips again.

She always seemed to have the power to soothe him, to erase his anger, to make him realise that things were not as black as they seemed. When the Prince dined with them alone, Gretna would retire as soon as dinner was over to give them a chance to talk together intimately. She was always careful that she did not intrude in any way on what was their so obvious happiness at being alone together.

Sometimes Maria would come up to her room to say good night to her after the Prince had left. But more often than not they would not meet again until the following morning.

It was one thing to chatter without formality with the Prince in Maria's house, but quite another to go to Carlton House Terrace and meet the Prince of Wales, heir to the Throne of Great Britain, the most envied and admired young man in the whole of Europe.

Gretna was longing to see Carlton House, but she had already learnt that the Prince's debts made it difficult for him to live there in the state he desired. In fact, she thought, lack of money was one of the topics of conversation which seemed always to crop up when the Prince was present, and she wondered how Maria could afford all the expenses of this big house which she had rented from Lord Uxbridge.

Even though she was rich with the wealth left to her by her last husband, the money that was expended at St. James's Square must exceed all she had received from Mr. Fitzherbert's will.

But it was difficult to feel worried about anything as she dressed that evening in what seemed to her the most wonderful gown she had ever seen. It was of white satin embroidered with tiny pearls and looped with bows of velvet ribbon sparkling with diamanté. Hoops had been discarded for less formal occasions, but Gretna learnt that they were still worn at Court and at Carlton House. But as if to offset the grandeur of the gown there were two pink roses caught at her breast which seemed to reflect the colour in her cheeks and the rosy tint of her lips.

Maria had debated for a long time whether her hair should be powdered or not, and to her surprise Gretna had insisted.

"It is not that I don't admire you for being brave enough to defy the fashion, dearest Maria, and wear your hair *au natural*," she said. "It is just that for my first evening at Carlton House, at any rate, I would like to be powdered."

"I am not certain it would not be cleverer to leave you as you are," Maria had sighed, but she had given in as Gretna was so insistent.

She was not to know that Gretna was frightened that the Marquis might be present and would recognise her. She could not guess that Gretna thought that powdered hair would make her disguise even more impenetrable in case, by any unfortunate chance, they should come face to face. And when finally she was ready, Maria admitted that she had been mistaken.

"You look exquisite," she exclaimed. "The powder shows off the clear loveliness of your skin, and it makes your eyes even bluer than they were before. You were right, my love, and I was wrong. Nothing could be more charming, nothing younger or more alluring."

There was no doubt that the company assembled at Carlton House thought the same. From the moment Gretna had entered the imposing Corinthian portico, passed through the marble hall and up the great staircase with its glittering gold balustrade, and had come to the magnificent State Apartments, she had been stared at and whispered about and quite unmistakably admired.

She had expected to find the Prince's own surroundings impressive, but she had not been prepared for the sheer splendour of them, for the huge, glittering chandeliers with the thousands of lighted tapers, for the rose satin hangings, the pictures, the rugs, the tapestries and everything in such perfect and undeniable good taste.

And the Prince himself, in the midst of it all, was exactly like the Prince Charming of the fairy-tales. He was so good-looking, so good-humoured, so gay and witty that it was not surprising that everyone seemed to hang spell-bound upon his slightest word.

But as Maria, with Gretna following her, appeared, he sprang forward with the eagerness of a schoolboy.

"We are indeed honoured that you should grace this gathering, Madam," he said to Maria, and there was no doubting the sincerity in his voice. And then he held out his hand to Gretna, raising her as she curtsied very low before him.

"Entrancing," he said for her ear alone, and then began to introduce her to his friends—the Duchess of Devonshire, Mrs. Crew, the Duke of Rutland, Lady Sefton.

Names were reeled off in a bewildering succession, faces swam before her eyes, and Gretna thought despairingly she would never remember who was who of the brilliant, elegant, important people to whom she curtsied.

And then she heard the Prince say:

"And here is another friend I should like to present to you. Someone who has been absent from our parties for far too long. The Marquis of Stade—Miss Gretna Hayden."

The moment had come; the moment she had dreaded. Gretna felt her heart give a startled leap. Just for a flashing second she glaced at the Marquis. She saw that his expression was severe, his eyes inscrutable, and then her dark eyelashes seemed to touch her cheeks as she sank down in a curtsy.

"Miss Hayden," the Marquis said slowly as if he was savouring the name, "I think we have met before."

There was a moment's silence and then Gretna raised her eyes and looked up at him. She had forgotten how tall he was, how magnificent.

"N . . . no, my Lord," she faltered. "You are . . . m . . . mistaken."

But even as she spoke, she saw by the expression in his eyes that he did not believe her.

6

GRETNA WAS HARDLY conscious of what happened next. She heard the Prince's voice introducing her to other people, to whom she curtsied automatically.

She heard vaguely, as if in the far distance, someone ask a question and her own voice replying in just the right tone of deference and a young girl's shyness. But all the time the blood seemed to be beating in her ears and her heart felt as if it must burst out beneath the soft satin of her gown.

The Marquis had recognised her! Her powdered hair, elegant dress and different background had not been enough to deceive him. His dark, penetrating eyes had looked into hers and seen the truth. She was the same girl who had fled into his arms from the unwelcome attentions of Lord Wroxhall at Stade Hall and whom he had kissed in the library of his house in Berkeley Square.

Afterwards Gretna had no knowledge of when the Prince's condescension in introducing her personally to his friends ended. She only knew that it seemed to her a long time until finally he took her back to Maria and said: "She will be *le dernier cri*, you may be sure of that," in a satisfied voice, as if he, himself, was her proud parent.

"Thank you, Sire, that was exceeding kind of you," Maria said softly, and a look passed between them which could only be exchanged between two people very much in love. Then Maria drew Gretna aside with a promise to show her some of the beauties of the Palace.

"You must see the Chinese Drawing Room," she said, then saw that Gretna was looking over her shoulder and asked: "You are seeking someone, my love?"

"No, no," Gretna said quickly, uncomfortably aware that she was lying and yet conscious that she could never tell Maria the truth.

The memory of what the Marquis had said about Maria came to her now and made her unduly perceptive as they moved amongst the brilliant, bejewelled people who crowded the Palace. There were smiles, compliments and many outstretched hands of greeting. But Gretna also saw people deliberately turn away as they approached, caught a glimpse of a sly look behind a dropped eyelid after a conventional remark had been made, and, occasionally, the lifting of a feminine chin and a look of disdain and disapproval in some elderly woman's eyes.

How hard it must be for Maria, she thought to herself, and drew a little closer as if, small as she was, she would protect her friend from the cruelty and the envy of those who resented her friendship with the Prince.

They went into the dining-room which was walled with silver and supported by columns of red and yellow granite. It was the most amazing room Gretna had ever seen, but Maria was more interested in telling her how clever the Prince had been to alter the domestic quarters of the Palace.

"Under his grandmother's—the Dowager Princess of Wales—regime the whole house was old-fashioned and out of date," she said, "and after she died, eleven years ago, it was allowed to become rat-infested, damp and mildewed. The staff quarters especially were dingy and horrible; but the Prince was determined that his servants should be comfortable. New kitchens have been built, sculleries, pantry, servants' hall and the maids' rooms, with proper ventilation—unlike the past when they had either suffocated or shivered."

"Poor things," Gretna exclaimed.

"He thinks always of other people," Maria said with a throb in her sweet voice, and Gretna could not help being impressed that a young man of twenty-four should have such a knowledge of what was necessary as well as the power to get such improvements made.

The food in the dining-room was delectable, but she was not hungry. She even refused a glass of champagne, to the consternation of several young dandies who had gathered round Maria and who tried to persuade her to change her mind.

They were engrossed in inspecting a boar's head stuffed and garnished in an entirely new manner, when Gretna managed to slip away without anyone noticing her departure. She thought it would be interesting to see the rest of the Palace and to give herself breathing space in which to collect her scattered thoughts and wonder, if she met the Marquis again, what she was to say to him.

There were so many people intent on enjoying themselves that no-one noticed her as she slipped between the chattering couples and wandered around, just looking at her surroundings. After a time she almost forgot the Marquis in her interest.

She found the drawing-room, hung with yellow silk and furnished in Chinese fashion. She passed through a dozen other rooms where brocades, velvets, satins, plush, *objets d'art*, porcelain and pictures all vied with each other for attention.

She was staring at a cabinet filled with miniatures, many of them having frames set with precious stones, when she heard a loud guffaw of laughter in the centre of the room.

"Have you seen the latest lampoon about her?" a voice asked.

She stiffened, realising instantly who was speaking. There was no mistaking that oily, sensual voice which somehow always had the power to send shivers down her spine.

She glanced round hastily and saw there were six or seven men, resplendent in their brocade coats, decorations and white breeches, gathered together beneath an enormous chandelier shaped like a water-lily. Then, realising that they had not noticed her amongst the other people perambulating the room, she stood staring at the glass case, afraid to move lest she should draw attention to herself.

"It's very funny of Mistress Fitz," Lord Wroxhall's hated voice went on, "and not too kind to our Prinny."

He obviously showed his cronies the lampoon, for there was a shout of laughter and then chuckles as if it was being passed from hand to hand, several of the men making, as they looked at it, somewhat obscene remarks which were, fortunately, spoken in too low a tone for Gretna to overhear what they said.

"Well, she certainly is in undisputed possession," someone remarked.

"I shouldn't be too sure of that," Lord Wroxhall replied.

"My dear fellow, you cannot argue against the evidence of one's own eyes. The Prince is absolutely infatuated with her—in fact, I have never seen him so in love before."

" 'Twill be but a passing phase," Lord Wroxhall remarked.

"I doubt that," someone else ventured. "Personally I find the fair Maria very charming. My wife refuses to acknowledge her, of course, which I hope will not come to the Prince's ears. He takes it ill if anyone does not accept her as if she were in reality his wife."

"I have never heard anything so nonsensical," Lord Wroxhall exclaimed. "And if the ladies who lead Society are prepared to have a piece of muslin foisted upon them, then it is time we men took a stand."

"It's all very well to talk like that," someone said. "But what can we do? You know as well as I do that if Mistress Fitzherbert is not invited to dine, then the Prince will not come either. We have to accept things as they are so long as she remains his favourite."

"So long as Mistress Fitzherbert remains," Lord Wroxhall said slowly. "Those, perhaps, are the words one should remember."

"Well, if you are going to try and get rid of her, old boy, you have set yourself a hard task," someone laughed.

"A hard task!" another man repeated. "An impossible one!"

"Nothing is impossible," Lord Wroxhall retorted. "Nothing"

"Well, I will lay you a wager," another voice chipped in. "A thousand to ten that you won't be rid of Mistress Fitzherbert before Christmas. You take it, Wroxhall?"

"I'll take and double it," Lord Wroxhall retorted.

There was something in the thickness of his voice that made Gretna sure he had been drinking. She longed to look round, to see to whom he was speaking, but she knew that if he caught sight of her the disguise might prove as ineffective where he was concerned as it had with the Marquis.

Carefully, keeping her back to the centre of the room, she moved along the walls, ostensibly looking at the pictures and at the statues in the alcoves, until she reached the door. Then with a little sigh of relief she ran as far as she could away from that particular Salon, putting almost the length of the Palace between her and that hated voice.

"How dare he?" she whispered to herself when finally she reached another Salon where a number of people were seated round baize-covered tables, playing cards. There was little noise here, only the chink of money, and quiet voices calling the winning card.

She felt herself suddenly hot with anger against Lord

Wroxhall. It was typical of him, she thought, that he should pretend to be a friend of the Prince and then decry Maria behind his back, making her more enemies amongst people who otherwise might have remained impartial.

She clenched her hands at the thought of his disloyalty. It was one thing which had always shocked her father, that anyone should be disloyal to a friend or should behave in a hypocritical manner, pretending affection where there was none.

"I hate him! I hate him!" Gretna muttered and, passing through the Salon, stepped outside on to a balcony which overlooked the garden where there was a fountain playing.

It was a warm night without a breath of wind. It had been extremely hot inside the Palace, for not only were there crowds of people, but the Prince insisted on having huge fires blazing in every room.

She stood and looked out on to the star-strewn sky, where a young moon was rising slowly, and felt her anger begin to ebb away. How big, how vast it all was, and for a moment she wondered why people should bother with such petty, trivial things as hatred and intrigue when there were all the beauties of the universe to charm them.

She heard somebody come out of the Salon behind her on to the balcony, but she did not turn her head. For a moment her thoughts were far away from the Palace and she was seeking eternity amongst the stars. Then a voice said quietly:

"I think you owe me an explanation.

She turned at that, her thoughts returning to the mundane world with a sense of shock. And then, as she saw who stood there, her fingers instinctively went to her breast as if she would kill the sudden leap of her heart.

The Marquis was looking magnificent tonight, she had to grant him that. He was wearing a coat of black velvet unrelieved except for a collar embroidered in pearls. Its severity made him seem unusually large and broad-shouldered and Gretna suddenly felt very small and vulnerable and altogether too weak to combat him.

She realised now that he had shut the window into the Salon behind him. They were alone on the balcony which became a small room in which they were entirely shut off from the rest of the world. The voices of the Prince's guests had faded into an indistinct hum and she could hear the splash and tinkle of the fountain below them in the garden.

She stood looking at the Marquis. The moonlight was on her face, showing that her eyes were dark with fear and her lips trembled a little as she answered:

"I must offer you my apologies, my Lord."

"Who are you?"

The question rang out almost like a pistol-shot, and because she felt she could elude him no longer Gretna told him the truth.

"M . . . my name is . . . G . . . Gretna Hayden."

"Who were your parents?"

She felt this was almost an inquisition and yet he had the power to compel her answer. She wanted to tell him it was none of his business, but almost in spite of herself the answer came dutifully from between her lips.

"My father was Captain William Hayden of the Grenadier Guards; my mother . . . L . . . Lady Rosemary Hayden."

"Lady Rosemary Hayden! You are sure of that?"

"Naturally I know my own mother's name," Gretna replied.

"I am interested and—surprised."

She felt herself stiffen at the smile on his lips, feeling it was somehow an insult to her mother. And then he said:

"So we are related."

"Related! How do you mean?" Gretna enquired.

"Unless I am mistaken, my grandmother and your grandmother were first cousins. That makes us—let me see—third or fourth cousins, but definitely related."

"I think you may be mistaken, my Lord."

"No, I am rather good when it comes to remembering my family tree. And I can recall—though I was only a boy at the time—the excitement your mother caused when she ran away from Avon the night before her wedding."

"My mother believed that . . . l . . . love was more important than anything else in . . . l . . . life," Gretna said with a little tremble in her voice.

"And you believe the same?"

She would have answered him, but a suspicion that perhaps he was laughing at her made her shy.

"I think my feelings on such a subject cannot be of interest . . . t . . . to you."

"As a matter of fact they interest me strangely," he said. "But we have other things to discuss for the moment, and as your kinsman I have a right to demand an explanation as to why you were masquerading as the niece of a fat farmer's wife."

Gretna looked down at the fountain in the garden, well aware that he was watching her profile and determined not to give him the satisfaction of seeing that she was afraid.

"It was all a . . . m . . . mistake," she said. "Mrs. Merryweather was kind enough to accompany me to London when I found I could no longer go on living in the cottage I had occupied with my parents when they were a . . . alive. When we had that accident, she thought it might be prejudicial to my good name to be travelling in such a manner and with no proper chaperon. You see, she had a rather poor opinion of . . . ge . . . gentlemen of quality."

The Marquis put back his head and laughed.

"And so, to save you from the attentions of such wolves in sheep's clothing, she presented you in a light which could not have been more damaging or reprehensible."

"Only to people like Lord Wroxhall and yourself," Gretna said hotly. "A girl from a farm should be able to travel without having the unwanted attentions of noblemen thrust upon her."

"An ordinary girl from a farm would undoubtedly be able to do so," the Marquis said coldly. "But then, the ordinary girl from a farm does not look like you."

"I think you are just making excuses for yourself, my Lord."

"On the contrary, I am making no excuses," the Marquis said. "You pretended to be what you are not. Whatever happened during that time was entirely your own fault. You invited it."

Gretna stamped her foot with a little gesture of impatience.

"All this would have been quite unnecessary if you had not recognised me," she said almost petulantly.

"Did you really think that I should not do so?" the Marquis asked. "You may have changed your gown and you have hidden the gold of your hair, but your face is just the same, and those troubled, innocent eyes of yours are quite unchanged."

"I think perhaps you are paying me a compliment, my Lord," Gretna said. "But I do not wish for your compliments or for those of Lord Wroxhall. If you will let me pass, I wish to return to the Salon."

She made a movement towards the window but the Marquis was blocking her way. She looked up at him and saw in the moonlight that cynical curve of his lips that she both feared and disliked.

"One minute," he said. "Do you not realise that I have been looking for you for the past three days? It was clever of you to leave my coach in Piccadilly and take a hackney carriage. Had I thought you would play such a trick, I should have gone with you."

"I see no reason why you should interest yourself in me," Gretna said. "And even if my deception gave you reason, now that you know who I really am there is no need for us to continue an acquaintanceship which should never have begun, save, perhaps, for the ill-judged t . . . tooling of your curricle."

She had the satisfaction of seeing the Marquis's eyes flash with a momentary anger.

"You are saying that to deliberately provoke me," he said slowly. "You have been very clever, but I am not to be sidetracked. Where are you staying? I wish to call on you."

"There is not the slightest . . . n . . . necessity, my Lord," Gretna replied "I am prepared to accept your Lordship's apology for the mistake that you made about me and excuse it on the grounds that you really imagined me to be a girl from a farm—a . . . m . . . milkmaid perhaps."

"Damme, I thought nothing of the sort," the Marquis said angrily. "Do you imagine that I am so blind and deaf and dumb that I did not realise that you had quality? I had best make myself very clear. I thought you to be the daughter of some nobleman who had perhaps not had the time, nor the inclination, to marry your mother. That is what I thought, and I think, even then, I suspicioned that the fat woman who accompanied you was no relation."

"Thank you for your frank explanation, my Lord Marquis," Gretna said, her eyes defying his and sparks seeming to flash between them. "I can only conclude that Mrs. Merryweather was absolutely right in mistrusting the nobility and doing her utmost to prevent me from dining alone with you."

"That is unfair," the Marquis said quickly. "I would not have hurt you and well you know it."

He paused a moment and added:

"And when I kissed you in my house in Berkeley

Square, it was only because Wroxhall's unwelcome attentions had made it seem imperative that I look after you."

His tone was quiet, but his words brought the blood flooding into Gretna's cheeks. They brought back all too vividly that moment when he kissed her and she had not resisted him and, indeed, had been unable to do so.

In her embarrassment she turned away, standing with her back to him to look out over the garden, again fighting for control, fighting, what was more, against a sudden desire to cry.

There was a long silence and then suddenly, in a very different tone, the Marquis said:

"Why are we quarrelling? Do you not realise, my dear, that you captivated me from the first moment that I set eyes on you?"

It must have been the sudden change in his tone, the unexpected tenderness, which brought the tears welling into Gretna's eyes and running unchecked down her cheeks. She made a little convulsive movement as if she would run away, although where she had no idea, and then he was beside her and his arms were round her shoulders.

"What have I done? What have I said that I should make you cry?" he asked. "Oh, my sweet, this is all so unnecessary."

"I . . . I am not . . . c . . . crying," Gretna said brokenly, trying to turn her head away so that he should not see.

"No?" he asked. "Then the stars have fallen out of the sky and are lying on your cheeks. Come, let me wipe them away."

She would have resisted him, but somehow she could not. Instead, she only closed her eyes, the big tears trembling on the end of her long lashes, and felt the softness of his lace-edged handkerchief wipe her cheeks.

He was very close. It was as if the bigness and strength of him enveloped her, and then she opened her eyes to see him looking down at her with an expression on his face she could not fathom.

"I . . . I must .. g . . . go," she said with a sudden frightened movement.

He did not move and she could not pass him.

"Are you running away from me?" he asked. "Or from your heart? I told you that I would make you love me, Gretna. It was a promise, not a threat."

"I shall never love you! N . . . never!" she said.

"Why must you be so vehement?" he asked. "And what have you against me?"

"It is impossible! You do not . . . understand," she answered.

"Tell me and try me," he begged.

"I . . . I cannot," she replied. "Let me go now, I beg of . . . you."

"You make it very difficult for me not to bully you," he said. "I want only to protect you and keep you safe from the world of which you are obviously completely ignorant. But always you are running away from me—first from Stade Hall, then from Berkeley Square and now, tonight. If I let you go, how shall I know that I shall find you again?"

"You must not try, that is the whole point," Gretna said. "We can mean nothing to each other. Our lives have crossed by accident, that is all. Forget me; forget that you ever met me. If we do meet again, pass me by as if you have never seen me before."

"Are you crazed?" he asked. "Can you imagine my doing such a thing? Do you not understand that I have dreamed of you since that moment when you emerged from the coach with a look of dismay on your face and yet it was still the loveliest face I have ever seen in my life?"

"Pray . . . do not say . . . any . . . more."

Gretna gave a little sob.

"But, why? Why should I not say it?" the Marquis enquired. "And I shall say the truth. From the moment that I kissed you in my house in Berkeley Square I knew that we belonged to each other, you and I."

"It is not true! It is not true!" Gretna said. "Please, let me go. I must go . . . now."

She pressed her hands against his chest as if by sheer strength she would force him away. He put his hands over hers and then, quite suddenly, she was very still. He held her there and through the quietness that fell between them she could feel the sudden beating of his heart.

She looked up at him. His eyes were clear in the moonlight and the expression in them made the world fall away from them both until they were utterly alone, caught between Heaven and earth, a man and a woman united with the fire of their feelings until they were one.

"How can you fight me?" he asked, his voice so low it

was hardly above a whisper. "How can either of us fight this?"

She was trembling and she had the strangest idea that he was trembling too. She knew suddenly that her parted lips were aching for his, that her whole body was yearning for the touch of his mouth, for the feeling that they were close and could come still closer to one another.

And then suddenly there was a loud laugh beneath them in the garden, the laugh of a man who has seen or heard something ribald. It broke the spell. Gretna moved convulsively, snatching her hands away, and instantly was free.

"I shall be missed," she said quickly. "I must return to . . . my friend."

"I will see you tomorrow," he said, still barring the way into the Salon.

"No," she said obstinately. "We shall not meet again."

"But I insist," he said. "You know as well as I do that we must see each other and that nothing and no-one shall prevent it."

"Let me pass . . ." Gretna pleaded.

"Only when you have told me where I can find you," the Marquis answered. "Although I dare say, if you refuse, the Prince would give me your address."

The last remark was almost a challenge, as if it was spoken because of some suddenly aroused suspicion within his breast.

"You can ask the Prince if you please," Gretna replied.

"But I would rather you told me," the Marquis answered. "What is this mystery? Are you betrothed, like your mother, to someone for whom you do not care? Are you even married?"

"Neither of those . . . things," Gretna answered.

"Then I see nothing of which I need be afraid," the Marquis said. "Stop playing and tell me where I may find you."

Gretna looked behind her and saw a man rise from one of the card-tables and come towards the window. She realised as he advanced that he was about to open it, obviously in need of fresh air. She paused for a moment and then almost despairingly, as a man might make a last pronouncement before the waters closed over his head, she said:

"You will find me, should you wish for further acquaintance, my Lord, at Lord Uxbridge's house in St. James's Square."

She saw the Marquis wrinkle his brow even as the window began to open and then, throwing back her head proudly, she said in a voice that was quite clear and unhesitant:

" 'Tis my friend's house. Her name is Mistress Fitzherbert!"

She saw the sudden stupefaction of the Marquis's expression, and then, as the card player opened the window, she stepped through it and into the Salon and was gone without looking back.

She hurried through the State apartments until, as she had expected, she found Maria beside the Prince. They were talking to a small circle of friends and as Gretna approached them Maria put out her hand and drew her close.

"I missed you, dearest," she said, "and I have sent innumerable young men in search of you. Where had you lost yourself?"

"I . . . I was admiring the pictures and . . . and the treasures of the Palace," Gretna stammered.

"I am gratified that they should prove so entrancing," the Prince said with a smile.

It was obvious that he was pleased and that any compliment to his house he took as a compliment to himself.

"I do hope it has not tired you," Maria said. "For I declare, you look quite pale. Shall we have a glass of wine or shall we retire? It is getting late."

"Please let us retire," Gretna pleaded.

Maria seemed to understand the urgency in her tone. She took leave of the Prince, curtsying to him with the utmost formality; but those standing immediately beside them could see how tightly he held her hand and realised that he whispered something in her ear.

Then she and Gretna were being escorted downstairs by one of the A.D.C.s who commanded a flunkey to find their carriage and handed them into it with a great show of politeness.

"What happened to you, my love?" Maria asked when at last they were alone and the coach was rumbling off towards St. James's Square. "When you came back to us, I would have vowed that you had seen a ghost."

Gretna was silent and after a moment she went on:

"I would not press your confidence, you know that. But it is obvious that you are troubled and I would wish to help you. I love you, Gretna. You really seem like a sister to me, and sisters should share everything, even unhappiness."

"You are so kind, so good to me," Gretna answered, feeling the tears come into her eyes again. "I would not wish to burden you with my troubles."

"It is no burden, dearest," Maria said. "But if anyone has made you unhappy, then I am ready to challenge them and, indeed, to fight them on your behalf."

"Oh, no," Gretna protested. "I would not have you fight anyone for me. You have so much to contend with, so many people against you, and you are so brave, so courageous. I admire you more than I can say, and I love you, too."

"And I love you," Maria said. "And therefore let there be no secrets between us."

Gretna had a great desire to throw herself into her friend's arms, to sob out everything that had happened since she left home. And yet she knew that it would be too unkind to repeat the cruel things that the Marquis had said, to reveal Lord Wroxhall's perfidy, and the wager he had taken. Such revelation would only hurt Maria and do no-one any good. She thought wildly for a moment what she could say, realising that to say nothing would also seem unkind and needlessly hurtful. At length the words came.

"I met a k . . . kinsman of mine tonight," she said. "He says that his grandmother and mine were first cousins. He claimed relationship and I think . . . I think he frightened me."

"It was quite unnecessary for him to do so," Maria retorted. "I know that your grandfather, the Earl of Ledbury, treated your mother disgracefully. I have never met the gentleman, but if I did I should feel like giving him a piece of my mind. But what business is it of this kinsman, whoever he may be, to take you to task? If, indeed, he has done so."

"I . . . I do not know," Gretna answered. "He appeared to interest himself in me, but I feel now that he will do so no more—in fact, I think it very unlikely that I shall ever see him again."

Even as she said the words Gretna felt her heart sink. Could it be true, she wondered for one second, that she minded? Would she, indeed, be glad if the Marquis went from her life and troubled her no further? She told herself hastily that she was glad, that she was sure that now he knew about her he would, in very truth, put her from his mind.

She could still hear the severity and force in his voice at Stade Hall as he spoke to Lord Wroxhall of his disgust and dislike of Maria. Was it likely, now he knew where she was staying, that he would call?

She wished she felt more elated at the prospect of being rid of him. She wished she was not conscious that the tears were running down her cheeks in the darkness of the carriage.

"Who is this man?" Maria was asking. "Do I know him?"

"I . . . I think . . . n . . . not," Gretna managed to answer.

"But what is his name?"

"His name is . . . the Marquis of . . . S . . . Stade," Gretna replied.

There was a moment's silence. She was well aware that the woman beside her had stiffened. And then in a voice of anger Maria said:

"That man! He is my most implacable, my most avowed, enemy!"

7

GRETNA AWOKE TO find Maria peeping round the bedroom door at her.

"You have slept late, dearest! I had not the heart to waken you until now," she said. "But we have a luncheon-party for twenty. If you do not rise now, you will be late, and that would never do, for, of course, the Prince is coming."

Gretna looked at the clock on the mantelshelf with dismay. It seemed that she had but closed her eyes for two minutes, having been awake until dawn. And yet now it was nearly luncheon-time.

She did not wish to explain that she had lain sleepless, tossing and turning, from the time they had returned from Carlton House, thinking over what had happened, going over again and again in her mind all that the Marquis had said.

"I am sorry, Maria," she apologised. "I will rise immediately."

"You must wear your prettiest gown," Maria said with a smile. "An old friend of yours is visiting us today."

She went from the room before Gretna had time to question her further. An old friend? She wondered who that could be, for she knew no-one in London save the Marquis, and she was quite certain that he would never cross the threshold of the house so long as Maria occupied it.

She felt again that leaden feeling that had been hers last night when she realised that she had, with one blow, severed all connection between them. He would no longer search for her, no longer wish to claim kinship now that he knew who the friend was whom she had sought so assiduously, now that he was aware of her address.

She put her hands up to her eyes for a moment as if not only to blot out the sunshine, which seemed for a moment to dazzle her eyes in which there was a suspicion of tears, but also to shut out the memory of the expression on the Marquis's face as she had last seen it.

It had only been a fleeting glance and yet, in that quick second, she had seen the darkening of his eyes, the tightening of his lips, and she had known that his reaction to her words had been exactly what she had expected.

Maria was her friend—she was also the woman he had denounced so violently and so vehemently at Stade Hall. She should be glad to be rid of him, she told herself, and wished that she did not feel so empty and as if something had gone from the whole joy of living.

"It is because I am tired," she said aloud, and looked in the mirror, expecting to find tell-tale lines under her eyes and an unusual pallor. Instead, her face looked back at her fresh and young and curiously untroubled, and almost petulantly she turned away from her own reflection.

It took her longer to dress than she had anticipated. The new gown which Maria had bought for her required a last-minute alteration and she was obliged to stand while the maid did it on her.

But when she was ready there was no doubt that the gown of forget-me-not blue satin was becoming. It had a white fichu brought round over the shoulders and tied in a large bow in the front, as was the very latest mode. There was a big black hat trimmed with pale blue feathers to go with the gown, but this she was not wearing for luncheon.

Instead, the maid brushed her hair until the last traces of powder were removed from it and then dressed it in curls high on her head so that they cascaded down the back, making her feel almost regal as she walked slowly down the broad staircase to the Salon.

She realised that she was late as she heard a sound of voices within, and felt suddenly shy of entering amongst the crowd of people who she felt would look at her critically. But she had no-one to blame but herself, so with a slight flush on her cheeks, which was due to embarrassment, she walked in to find several ladies seated while a number of gentlemen, very elegant in their tail-coats and tight white breeches, conversed with them as they sipped a glass of wine.

For a moment Gretna stood hesitant in the doorrway, and then Maria looked up and saw her.

"Ah! Here you are, dearest," she said. "I was just wondering what could have delayed you. Let me present you to my friends."

She took Gretna by the hand and presented her to each lady in turn. Gretna curtsied demurely and knew by the gracious condescension of each head that she was accepted.

It was then the turn of the gentlemen and while they each made her a most elegant bow, Gretna was puzzling her brain as to which was likely to prove an old friend when another name was announced by the butler from the doorway.

"Sir Harry Carrington."

Gretna gave a definite start of surprise as Maria went forward with her hand outstretched.

"Sir Harry, I am so pleased to see you," she said to the young gallant whom Gretna had last seen at Stade Hall. "And here is someone whom you told me last night you were very anxious to meet again—my dear friend, Miss Gretna Hayden."

Sir Harry bowed and then said eagerly:

"Indeed, I was so consumed with anxiety to renew our acquaintance, that was why I besought Mistress Fitzherbert to invite me here today."

"How did you know who I was?" Gretna asked.

He looked surprised at the question.

"Had a glimpse of you, of course, last night at Carlton House. Did you think you would not be recognised?"

"I am afraid my disguise was not as good as I had

hoped," Gretna answered a little ruefully, remembering all too vividly that the Marquis had not been deceived either.

"I tried to speak to you," Sir Harry said. "But you disappeared in the crowd and hunt as I would I could not find you again. But I had seen you arrive with Mistress Fitzherbert and so I told her how much I desired to find you and she was gracious enough to invite me here to-day."

"It all sounds very simple," Gretna smiled, and then in a low voice so no-one could overhear her she said: "Did you tell Mistress Fitzherbert where we met?"

"I'm no gabster," Sir Harry answered. "And there was such a crush at Carlton House that it was difficult to utter a coherent sentence. I merely said I had met you before and greatly desired to do so again."

Gretna gave a little sigh of relief.

"Pray say nothing about Stade Hall," she said. "I will explain why later."

It was, indeed, very much later that she had a chance to say anything to Sir Harry. The Prince did not like hurrying over his meals, which were, Gretna discovered, invariably very elaborate, and it was after three o'clock before any of them rose from the dining-table.

Then Maria wished to drive in the Park and although Sir Harry offered to accompany them there was no chance of speaking in private with him.

It was only when they returned home and it was obvious that now was the moment for him to make his farewells that Maria left them in the Salon while she went to interview someone who had called to solicit her help. As she shut the door behind her, Gretna said a little shyly:

"You must think it strange of me, Sir Harry, to ask you not to mention where we first met. B . . . but the . . . M . . . Marquis is not a f . . . friend of Mistress Fitzherbert."

Sir Harry looked a little uncomfortable at that and Gretna knew at once that he was well aware of the Marquis's sentiments where Maria was concerned.

"I would not say anything to embarrass you," he remarked.

"Maria will not ask questions," Gretna said. "And I presume that you did not believe that Mrs. Merryweather, the farmer's wife who was accompanying me in the stage-coach, was really my aunt."

"I'm not mutton-headed," Sir Harry replied. "I thought it a hum from the moment she said it. You were far too beautiful to be connected in any way with a farm—nasty, dirty places I always think."

Gretna laughed at that and suddenly they were both laughing, two young people amused more by the sheer adventure of living than because anything was particularly funny.

"When shall I see you again?" Sir Harry asked, and there was no mistaking his eagerness.

"You know where I am living," Gretna replied demurely.

"You will permit me to call?"

"I am always very pleased to see ... old friends," Gretna answered.

Even as she spoke the words she thought she was, indeed, glad to see Sir Harry. He was young and gay and there was nothing complicated in her relationship towards him. They could laugh at the same things. He was easy to talk to and never would he make her feel afraid, as the Marquis did.

"I shall never forgive Stade for turning me away that evening and making me go to a ball which turned out to be a dead bore," Sir Harry said. "I give you my word that I have thought about you ever since, and when I saw you last night I could hardly believe my luck."

"I still think it was very clever of you to recognise me."

"I could not forget you, and that's the truth," Sir Harry vowed.

There was no doubting his sincerity and when Gretna held out her hand to him he raised it to his lips.

"I will be here tomorrow," he said. "That is if we do not meet tonight, as I expect we shall."

"Tonight?" Gretna queried.

"Yes, indeed," he replied. "Mistress Fitzherbert told me that she has a dinner-party and that you are all going on afterwards to a gaming party given by the Duchess of Devonshire."

"Oh, are we?" Gretna said. "I had no idea."

"If there is dancing—and there usually is at Devonshire House—will you dance with me?" Sir Harry asked.

Gretna was just about to answer him when Maria came into the room. She looked slightly surprised to find Sir Harry still there and he made his adieu rather quickly and went away.

Maria touched Gretna's cheek with her hand.

"So you have made a new conquest," she said. "He is a charming boy."

"But only a boy," Gretna answered.

"Well, I am sure he says nice things to everyone, but particularly nice ones to you," Maria smiled.

She sat down in her chair and opened the marquetry work-box which stood beside it and drew out her embroidery.

"It is delightful to have a few moments to ourselves," she said. "I seem to get so little time for my needlework these days. It would be pleasant, dearest, if you would read to me. We could choose a book that we both enjoy."

"I should like that," Gretna said. "But I wonder if you would think that I read well enough."

"I am sure you read beautifully," Maria Fitzherbert answered. "You have a sweet voice just like your mother's. I always thought one of the most attractive things about Lady Rosemary was her voice."

"If it comes to that," Gretna answered, "my father once said that you had a voice like a nightingale that had been fed on honey."

Maria clapped her hands together.

"What a splendid compliment," she said. "And from your father, who never paid one unless he really meant it. I had the deepest admiration for him, you know. When he was so ill he never complained. I think it was because he loved your mother too much to distress her with his sufferings."

"They were happy together, weren't th . . . they?" Gretna said with a little sob in her voice. "They lived a very quiet life with no money and very few friends, and yet I do not think they would have changed places with anyone."

"They were the luckiest people I know," Maria Fitzherbert answered. "Neither money nor friends are necessary to love if two people love enough and can be together."

There was no mistaking the wistfulness in the last two words and Gretna suddenly stepped forward and knelt down beside her friend's chair.

"It must be very difficult for you," she whispered softly.

"It is, because we cannot always be together," Maria answered. "And when we are, there are always people there too. The most precious of all the moments to be treasured are when we are alone—and there are so few of them."

She bent her head and then raised it again and Gretna saw that her eyes were like tear-drenched violets.

"Would it not be best to go away and forget him?" Gretna asked almost in a whisper.

It was the pain on her friend's face which gave her the courage to speak the words. Maria looked at her for a moment incredulously and then she said:

"Oh, no! You do not understand, I love him and he loves me. That is all that matters. Any suffering is worth while because of that; any discomfort; any insults. It is all of little consequence beside the greatness of our love."

There was almost the sound of rapture in her tones and Gretna felt there was nothing she could say. Yet she could not help a prayer in her heart that Maria would never be disappointed or hurt by the man she loved. The Prince was so young, so gay, so surrounded by alien influences. She had thought privately there could be nothing more frightening than to love him or even be loved by him.

Maria suddenly drew her down and kissed her cheek.

"It is so wonderful for me to have you here," she said softly. "And now, dearest, find a book and read to me, for if we talk of ourselves my work will not only never be finished, it will never be begun."

She took up her embroidery frame resolutely as she spoke and Gretna picked up the books which stood on a side-table and read out their titles one by one. "Is this Miss Burney's latest novel?" she asked. "I would love to read that."

"Then start it right away," Maria suggested. "I find Miss Burney's tales entrancing and Sir Joshua Reynolds told me he sat up all night to read *Evelina.*"

Gretna settled herself in the corner of the sofa. She was glad that Maria had not chosen one of the classics or a book with erudite, unusual words over which her tongue would trip. She had often read aloud to her father, but this was something different; and though she loved Maria, she was very conscious of how much cleverer and better educated the older woman seemed.

"Cecilia or Memoirs of an Heiress by Fanny Burney," she read aloud. "Volume II, Chapter One."

She got no further before the door opened and the butler said:

"There is a gentleman here, Madam, who wishes to see you alone if it is convenient. He says it is of the utmost importance."

"And what is his name?" Maria asked.

"The Marquis of Stade, Madam."

Gretna gave a little gasp and dropped the book she was holding on to the floor. It fell with a dull thud. She let it lie and turned to look at Maria. For a moment there was a pause; then Maria said in a firm and resolute tone:

"Will you show the Marquis in."

"No, Maria! No!" Gretna said, only to be silenced by an almost imperious wave of Maria's hand.

"I must see him," she said. "There is nothing to be gained by not hearing what he has to say."

They sat in silence, though Gretna could hear the pounding of her heart, until the door opened again and the butler announced:

"The Marquis of Stade!"

He entered the room, looking more grim and formidable, Gretna thought, than usual. She found it hard to look at him, hard to rise to her feet, which had suddenly become unsteady, and sink down in the conventional curtsy as he bowed first to Mistress Fitzherbert and then to her.

"I hope you will pardon my intrusion, Madam," he said, and his voice was hard and his words conventional though they seemed to be spoken with an icy coldness which made Gretna feel as if she must shiver.

He had advanced as he spoke and now stood near to Maria and almost facing herself, and vaguely, with one less frightened part of her brain, Gretna noticed the exquisite cut of his dark blue cloth coat and how the unusual severity of it made him seem larger and more imposing than usual. His hessian boots were polished until one could see the furniture reflected in them and the snowy whiteness of his breeches was echoed only by the crispness of his cravat.

He should have looked a dandy, Gretna thought wildly, and instead he seemed merely strong and terrifying, a man who could frighten her more than anyone she had ever met in her life before.

"Is there anything I can do for you, my Lord?" Maria was asking in her soft, melodious voice and in a quite unhurried manner as if she was not the least perturbed by this sudden instrusion.

"I have come to request, Madam, that my young cousin, Miss Gretna Hayden, shall accompany me to the house of my grandmother, the Dowager Marchioness of Stade, who will be delighted to offer her hospitality for so long as she wishes to remain in London."

Gretna gave an exclamation of surprise. Maria ignored it.

"That is most generous of your grandmother," she said quietly. "But Gretna has only just arrived to visit me and I am glad of her company."

"That I can well believe, Madam," the Marquis said in a voice heavy with sarcasm. "But if you will pardon my presumption, I think my cousin's interests would be best served if she visited those to whom she is related by birth."

"That, of course, must be for Gretna to decide," Maria replied. "I have told her that she can make her home here when she wishes and for as long as she wishes. If she desires to go to the Dowager Marchioness, then I shall, of course, be reluctant to part with her, but I will respect her wish."

"But I do not want to go away," Gretna said hotly.

Maria, who had seated herself after curtsying to the Marquis, rose to her feet. She turned her back on him and taking Gretna's face between her two hands looked down into her eyes.

"You must do what is best," she said softly. "Whatever your choice may be, I shall understand."

She kissed Gretna on the forehead, then turning again to the Marquis said:

"I will leave you, my Lord, to discuss this with Gretna. It is her interests which are at stake. You will understand that I would not wish to influence her one way or the other."

Gretna thought there was a look of surprise in the Marquis's face as if Maria's gentle dignity was something he had not expected. And then he crossed the room to open the door for her as she went, her soft satin skirts billowing out around her as she moved.

Gretna stood very still save that her small fingers twisted each other together. The Marquis closed the door and came back to the hearthrug to face her.

"It would be best for you to pack your box immediately," he said.

Gretna took a deep breath.

"Do you really believe I would go with you?" she asked.

"But, of course," he answered. "It is not correct for you to stay here."

"Not correct!" Gretna repeated. "That comes strangely from you, my Lord. You made, I think, very different suggestions as to what hospitality I should enjoy when I first came to London."

"That episode was, I hoped, forgotten," the Marquis answered. "It was unfortunate, exceedingly unfortunate, but it was brought about, I may remind you, by a very stupid deception that you practised at our first meeting. Had you told the truth, then you would not now be staying in this house."

"A house where I am very happy, where I have been invited by a friend whom I have known all my life and who has befriended not only me, but both my father and my mother," Gretna retorted.

"I am not denying anything that has happened in the past," the Marquis answered. "In fact, I see no reason why we should argue about anything. My grandmother has invited you to stay with her at her house in Richmond."

"And why this sudden interest in me?" Gretna asked. "I shall be eighteen next birthday and this is the first time in the whole of my life that your grandmother—or any other relation—has invited me under her roof. Why this interest? And how, indeed, did she know of my existence?"

"She knew because I rode to Richmond this morning and told her that we had met and where you were at present residing," the Marquis answered. "She instantly extended you an invitation to visit her for as long as you wished."

"Then perhaps you will be k . . . kind enough to convey my . . . c . . . compliments to your grandmother, the Dowager Marchioness," Gretna answered, "and thank her for her kind but . . . b . . . belated invitation. Tell her that I hope we shall meet while I am in London, but that I am already previously engaged to stay with my d . . . dear friend Mistress Fitzherbert."

Gretna had spoken a little hesitantly as she started, but by the time she had finished her voice was firm and her eyes met the Marquis's squarely. She saw his lips tighten, the sudden squaring of his jaw, and knew that he was incensed with her. He answered quietly enough.

"I am afraid I must insist that you accompany me."

Her eyebrows went up at that.

"Insist?" she queried. "On what grounds?"

"I am your cousin."

"A very distant one," she interposed.

"Nevertheless, a blood relative, and high in seniority when it comes to family affairs. I hesitate to say this, but I do not consider the environment of this house suitable to a young girl."

"What you think does not carry the slightest weight with me," Gretna said, feeling her anger mount at the calm assumption of the Marquis that he could speak with such authority as if she was only a slave or a chattel who must obey his wishes.

"My mother was cast off by your family because she married the man she loved. She died in great poverty. I was turned out of my house and had nowhere to go, but none of my smart, rich relations, who are suddenly appearing from n . . . nowhere, were worried about me any more than they w . . . worried about my m . . . mother."

Her voice faltered for a moment, then she continued:

"I have my friends who have stood by me in trouble. It is th . . . they who should be allowed to dictate what I shall do and what I shall not d . . . do."

She spoke passionately, but it seemed as if her words had made little impact on the Marquis. He still regarded her coldly until suddenly, when she least expected it, he smiled and held out his hand.

"We are quarrelling again," he said. "Don't be nonsensical, Gretna. Let me take you to my grandmother."

A moment or two earlier he might have beguiled her, but now she was too angry.

"I am staying here with Mistress Fitzherbert," she said. "I know what you think about her—as it happens, I overheard what you said to Lord Wroxhall at Stade Hall. But you admitted then that you had never met her. If you knew her, if you were with her for only a little while, you would not be able to believe that she is capable of any of the things of which you accuse her."

The Marquis hesitated for a moment and then he said:

"I do not want to argue, Gretna. Come and stay with my grandmother and we will talk it over on another occasion."

"I have no intention of leaving here," Gretna answered. "I am happy, very happy, and Maria has been more kind to me than I would have believed possible. Why, she has given me everything—a home, lovely clothes, this very gown I have on. Can you imagine that I should be so ungrateful as to walk out just because someone arrives with what they consider a better invitation?"

"I am not doubting Mistress Fitzherbert's kindness to you," the Marquis said. "And any money she has expended on your behalf shall be repaid."

"By whom?" Gretna asked quickly.

"I will repay it," he answered.

"Do you imagine she would accept your money?" Gretna demanded. "Or that I would permit you to pay for my gowns? Really, my Lord, you take upon yourself too much. After all, I have only your word for it that you are my cousin—and, when it comes to that, that you are taking me to your grandmother and not to some little house in Ch . . . Chelsea, with a c . . . carriage of my o . . . own!"

"You are being childish and ridiculous," the Marquis said angrily.

"And you are being overbearing and in . . . insulting," Gretna retorted.

They stood glaring at each other and the Marquis said, with an obvious effort at self-control:

"This is absurd. You know as well as I do that my invitation from my grandmother is genuine. She would have written to you had I not been in such a hurry and her hands are often stiff with rheumatism in the early morning. If you insist, I will ride back to Richmond and get a letter inviting you to stay with her."

"There is no need to put yourself about," Gretna answered. "As I have already told you, I have no intention of leaving here and going to stay with your grandmother, or with anyone else."

"I do not want to say this," the Marquis said almost between his teeth, "but you force it from me. This is not a proper or respectable house for an innocent girl. If you stay here with the Prince's mistress, then you lay yourself open to insults and to aspersions on your character which you will find it hard to bear and still harder to refute."

He spoke slowly and in a manner which made his words seem even more weighty and overwhelming than they would have done if he had spoken in anger.

"You have no r . . . right to make such a . . . assertions," Gretna answered in a low voice.

"Unfortunately they are true," the Marquis said.

Gretna turned towards the window and stood there for

a moment looking out on to the trees in the Square, and the sunshine and the coaches moving slowly past. After a moment she said:

"And suppose the Prince is, in reality, married to Mistress Fitzherbert. Would you not then be ashamed of your w . . . words?"

"He is not married to her," the Marquis said quietly.

"How can you be sure of that? You say yourself you have never met her until today. I have lived in this house. I have seen how he treats her. I have seen the love he bears for her and, more than that, the respect, almost amounting to reverence, which he shows her on every possible occasion. Is that the behaviour of a man with his m . . . mistress? I know nothing of these m . . . matters, but it is not what I should have expected or believed would have occurred between a man and woman who are not joined together by something greater than . . . passion."

Gretna almost whispered the last words, and she saw that the Marquis was listening intently, his brows knit as if he strove to follow her reasoning. Then he replied:

"You speak very convincingly, Gretna. I might even be inclined to believe you if it were not for one thing."

"What is that?" Gretna asked.

"The Prince himself has denied the marriage," the Marquis answered.

"I do not believe it," Gretna said. "When has he made any such denial?"

In answer the Marquis put his hand in his breast pocket and drew out a letter.

"I promised to show this to no-one," he said. "But I am going to break my word because I consider the circumstances justify my using any means in my power to take you away from here. This is a letter written by the Prince to Charles James Fox. You have heard of him I am sure. A great politician, a man to whom the Prince has, in my opinion, very wisely entrusted his friendship."

"I think I met him last night," Gretna murmured.

"He was there," the Marquis answered. "And if anyone could obtain the truth on such a question as the Prince's marriage, it would be Mr. Fox."

He turned the letter over in his hands, then opened it.

"Charles Fox wrote to the Prince last December when the first wild rumours of his marriage to Mistress Fitzherbert began to circulate all over London. He stressed the damage of His Royal Highness's rights to the Crown if he married a Roman Catholic. He even went on to say that if it took place it could not even be a legal marriage."

The Marquis paused, looked down at the letter in his hand and then held it out to Gretna.

"Here is the Prince's reply," he said, "to his closest friend, a man whom he has always trusted."

Gretna took the letter from him with trembling hands. For a moment she considered whether it would be better not to read it, and then she thought it would be merely childish to refuse. For a moment the writing danced before her eyes, then she read it slowly down to the last word.

My dear Charles,

Your letter of last night afforded me more satisfaction than I can find words to express, as it is an additional proof to me (which I assure you I did not want) of your having that true regard and affection for me which it is not only the wish but the ambition of my life to merit. Make yourself easy, my dear friend. Believe me, the world will soon be convinced that there not only is not, but never was any ground for these reports, which of late have been so malevolently circulated. I have not seen you since the apostasy of Eden . . . Believe me at all times, my dear Charles, most affectionately yours,

George P.

Carlton House,
Sunday Morning 2 o'clock December 11, 1785.

As Gretna finished reading the letter she felt as if someone had given her a sharp blow. Her heart felt leaden and her lips were dry.

She folded the letter together and passed it back to the Marquis. She turned again to the window, her back towards him. There was a moment's pregnant silence and then the Marquis said in a matter-of-fact tone:

"My carriage is waiting. How long will it take you to be ready?"

Gretna closed her eyes. It seemed to her as if her throat was constricted. She felt, too, as if the whole world waited for her answer—the world that she had known; a small world, but nevertheless her own. And then, quite clearly it seemed to her, she heard her father saying:

"There is nothing more despicable than a man or a

woman who change their loyalties merely through force of circumstance."

Loyalty was little to the mind, but everything to the heart. That was the answer. That was what she wanted to know. There was no longer any difficulty in making her decision. She turned round and faced the Marquis.

"I am not going with you," she said simply. "I am staying here with Maria. She needs me."

The Marquis's eyes met hers. She saw the anger and what seemed to her the disdain in them before she dropped her head and her eyelashes swept her cheek as the colour rose in a crimson flood.

Something boiled up inside her, something which made her lose control of herself. Her chin went up and she faced the Marquis defiantly. Before she could prevent the words, they burst from her lips:

"G . . . Go away," she stormed. "You s . . . spoil everything, besmirch e . . . everything. I was h . . . happy and now it is all s . . . spoiled. I h . . . hate you—yes, h . . . hate you!"

The Marquis bowed. It was an ironical bow that somehow managed to turn what was a courtesy into an insult.

"I think," he said slowly, "that you will be well suited to the life you have chosen."

Gretna met his eyes. She felt the fire in his was echoed in her own. She watched him cross the room, saw the door open and close behind him. Only when she heard him descending the stairs did she know that he had gone beyond recall.

And it was then, as she stood there trembling as if from the impact of some almost overwhelming violence, she knew that she loved him—loved him with her whole heart—now that it was too late!

8

IT SEEMED TO Gretna that for the next few weeks there was never a moment when she was not at a party or getting ready to go to a party. Everyone said that the

London Season of 1786 was one of the most unusual and brilliant gaiety that had been seen for years.

Gretna was quite prepared to believe it. The King and Queen, having more or less abdicated all the functions of the Court, spent their time in a lonely isolation at Buckingham House. Society looked, therefore, to the Prince of Wales to give a lead, and accompanied by Mistress Fitzherbert he went from Ball to Masque, from Assembly to Rout, until Gretna's impressions were so chaotic that she found it difficult to remember whom she had met or which person was more distinguished than the last.

The speed at which she was living made it hard for her to find time to think about herself. And yet she was unceasingly conscious of an ache somewhere in her heart which would not be assuaged.

At first, after the Marquis had left the Salon with that look of disdain and coldness in his face, she was afraid of meeting him again. And then she began to be afraid that she never would meet him again, for he seemed to have disappeared from the London scene.

She would find herself thinking she saw him amongst the brilliant, colourful crowd moving up the staircase at Carlton House, or in the throng which filled the drawing-room on a Sunday evening at the French Embassy, and her heart would give a sudden leap and seem to turn over in her breast—only to find she had been mistaken. It was not the Marquis's severe, proud face that she saw, and the eyes that met hers were not dark and penetrating and disdainful, but, instead, full of admiration.

"I am happy. I have never been happier," Gretna told Maria, and tried to convince herself that it was true.

She found it hard to talk to Sir Harry Carrington about the Marquis without revealing how interested she was. Sir Harry was always at her side now and seldom an evening passed when he did not either dine with them in St. James's Square or accompany them to the house of some brilliant hostess.

"I asked your young man specially because he begged me to do so," the Duchess of Rutland said with a smile when she told Gretna that Sir Harry was to take her down to supper.

And the beautiful Duchess of Devonshire, whose action in kissing the butcher to gain a vote for Mr. Fox was still talked about and depicted in cartoons, asked: "When are we going to come to your wedding, little one? I have already a very charming present in mind for you."

Gretna managed to blush and say nothing, but she could not ignore the fact that Sir Harry was desperately in love with her and was making no pretence of hiding his affection.

She liked him; she liked him so much that she even played a little with the idea of accepting the offer of marriage which she knew he would make to her at the first convenient moment. Then she thought of the love that her father and mother had borne each other and knew that any affection she could feel for Sir Harry would be but a very pale pretence of the passion which had made her parents inseparable even in death.

"Harry, it is so enjoyable being able to converse with you," she said to him one evening when they were dancing together at a masked ball given by Mrs. Sheridan, "that I realise how much I have missed in never having had a brother."

"Damme!" Harry Carrington ejaculated. "I don't want to be a brother to you, Gretna."

"That is how I think of you," she said firmly.

"I love you, you know that well enough," he said ardently.

She shook her head at him, well aware that she was looking her best with her hair powdered and embellished with two pink roses. She wore a gown of blush-pink satin covered with a pink gauze—a material which had crossed the Channel only a week previously.

"You are becoming a minx," Sir Harry warned her. "If you are not careful, the hostesses will be talking of you as a flirt, and then you will be finished, my girl."

"Why should that shock them?" Gretna asked in surprise. "There are a great many people in this room who flirt, I have seen them at it."

"But you must be particularly careful not to get a bad reputation," Sir Harry said, and then pressed his lips together as if he felt he had said too much.

There was no need for him to say more. Gretna was well aware of the insinuation behind his words. She, above all other girls of her age, must be circumspect, because of the situation in which she found herself, because she was living in the same house as Maria Fitzherbert.

It was all too obvious. The little innuendoes, the half-spoken remarks of people, even the look in an eye which told her that, while Society accepted Mrs. Fitzherbert because the Prince of Wales insisted on it, they were still only too ready to condemn the relationships between the Heir to the Throne and the attractive Roman Catholic widow. What was more, they would be delighted, if the winds veered in the wrong direction, to transfer their allegiance back again to the stolid respectability of Buckingham House.

That night Gretna, trying to forget the Marquis, had a reminder of him which she least expected. She was passing along a corridor towards the ballroom on Sir Harry Carrington's arm when they met a formidable old lady advancing towards them. She was not very tall and she walked with an ivory-handled stick, but her magnificent diamonds were of the first water. Her dazzling tiara and the brilliants round her neck made Gretna stare, almost forgetful of her manners, when the old lady stopped abruptly.

"Harry Carrington!" she said in a voice that seemed to come almost whistling between her lips. "And do not deny it! You're the spitting image of your father at your age."

"Indeed, I am Harry Carrington, at your service, Ma'am," he replied, bowing courteously.

"I was convinced of it. And as wild as your father, I presume?"

"Indeed, no, Ma'am! I could not attempt to level up to his flights," Sir Harry answered laughingly.

"No, I expect you couldn't," the Dowager replied. "The modern generation are a mealy-mouthed lot and not up to snuff compared with their parents. Who's this pretty wench you're taking in to supper?"

She pointed her stick at Gretna who curtsied politely.

"May I present Miss Gretna Hayden, Ma'am?" Sir Harry said hastily—"the Dowager Marchioness of Stade."

The Marchioness raised a quizzing glass to look Gretna over.

"So you're the chit who refused my invitation," she said.

Gretna felt the colour rise in her cheeks. She had not expected that the Marquis's grandmother would be anything so formidable as the old lady facing her. And yet now she began to see a likeness in the straight features and in the proud carriage of the head.

"It was very gracious of you to invite me, Ma'am," she said. "Unfortunately I had already accepted an invitation to stay with my friend, Mistress Fitzherbert."

"So I understand," the Dowager answered, and Gretna realised that she had known all along who she was and wanted, perhaps out of curiosity, to speak with her.

"Nevertheless, I must thank you, Ma'am, for the kind thought," Gretna said a little breathlessly.

"You are like your mother," the Marchioness said. "Determined to have your own way. Well, I dare say it did my grandson no harm to be thwarted for once. Too pampered and too spoiled, that's what these bachelors are these days, eh, Sir Harry?"

"Yes, Ma'am. Of course, Ma'am," Sir Harry said, eager to agree with her. And then added quickly: "Not that Julien is that way. Always thinking of other people from what I have seen of him."

"Only so long as they agree with him," the Dowager snapped. "But loyalty is not a bad virtue. It's quite right for you to stick up for your friend, Harry Carrington. It's the sort of thing your father would have done."

She spoke to Harry, but she looked at Gretna. And then, as she passed on her way, Gretna felt with certainty that she had won that august lady's approval when she had least expected it.

"Phew! I didn't think we would run into her," Sir Harry said in the tones of a boy who had just come through a gruelling interview with his headmaster.

"She is very frightening," Gretna said.

"Frightening! I'd rather face a firing squad any day than pass an hour with the old lady. Julien used to have her to stay at Stade Hall and force Harriet and me to dine and entertain her. We always used to make all sorts of excuses to avoid going, but he would insist!"

Gretna could guess how determined the Marquis would be.

"They were pretty difficult dinner-parties I can tell you," Sir Harry went on. "At the same time, the old lady's got a sense of fun. The stories she used to tell me about my father in his young days made him furious when he heard about them."

"Was she gay?" Gretna asked.

"Gay!" Sir Harry prepeated. "She was the reigning toast. Had the whole place by the ears because of her carryings on. She's always twitting Julien with being too staid and pompous. Invariably she sets him down a peg. She's about the only person who can do it, I can tell you that."

"Is the Marquis so formidable then?" Gretna enquired.

"At times he's a devil!" Sir Harry confessed. "You know what a friend he has been to me and how much I admire him. But when he's angry, well, he's pretty nearly as bad as his grandmother—and that's something I don't like to think about."

Gretna felt herself shiver. If the Marquis was angry with her, then what hope had she of assuaging his wrath or even persuading him to forget it, when his very friends were afraid of him? She wished, for some obscure reason which she could not even explain to herself, that she could have a talk with the Dowager Marchioness. She did not know why, but she felt that she would like to hear more from her about her grandson. Then she knew that such an idea was impossible.

That night when they got home from the party Maria put her arm round Gretna's shoulder and said:

"You look tired, dearest. Have you been doing too much lately?"

"No, indeed!" Gretna answered. "It is just that it was rather hot and I do not think I enjoyed the ball so much tonight as I have on other occasions."

"You are getting blasé," Maria teased; and then when Gretna would have protested she said: "It is true of all of us. We can all have too much of a good thing. I enjoy the parties we go to; but oh, how I long for a quiet evening at home, a night when we could sit and talk about ourselves and perhaps listen to a little music."

She spoke wistfully and Gretna knew that she was not thinking of an evening when they might be together, two girls chattering and laughing over their parties, but of being alone with the Prince.

"Why do you not arrange such an evening?" she asked rather daringly. "Surely His Royal Highness would sometimes like to be quiet?"

Maria shook her head so that her golden curls danced in the light of the candelabra.

"No, indeed! The Prince is young and quite insatiable where amusement is concerned. He loves every minute, not so much of the parties, but of the people whom he meets. I think the truth is, Gretna, that he enjoys the company of brilliant men and the society of beautiful women."

Maria smiled as she spoke and Gretna was well aware of something a little wistful behind the smile. "It must be hard," she thought, "to love someone as deeply as Maria loves the Prince and be alone with him so little."

Upstairs in her room she found herself thinking, as she had thought so often before, of the situation which existed between Maria and the Prince and wondering what, indeed, was the truth. Although no-one had ever been ill-bred enough to question Gretna on the subject, she was well aware that they longed to do so.

She could almost see the words trembling on some fashionable lady's lips and then being bitten back almost as they were spoken; and Gretna wondered, if anyone did ask her what was the truth, what she would say. For, indeed, she had no idea herself whether they were married or not married.

It seemed impossible that Maria Fitzherbert should allow herself to become the butt of coarse jokes, to be depicted in lampoons and to lay herself open to the insults which she invariably suffered from time to time, if she was not, in fact, sustained and fortified by the secret knowledge that she was, indeed, the legal wife of the man she loved.

And the Prince treated her always with a delicate deference which, in itself, appeared to be a recognition of her unique position. His good manners were proverbial; it was not for nothing that people spoke of him as the "First Gentleman in Europe"; and he never forgot to pay her the courtesy at the end of a party of saying: "Madam, may I have the honour of seeing you home in my carriage?"

And at home, while his adoration showed itself in a thousand ways and in expressions of the deepest and most profound affection, he still took none of the liberties nor indeed behaved with any of the familiarity which might have been expected from a man off his guard in the house of his mistress.

"Is it true or is it not true that they are wed?" Gretna asked herself as she sat down on her bed, and then she remembered the bitter voice of the Marquis and his words: "I feel, Madam, that you are admirably suited to the life you have chosen."

She had never heard greater contempt in any voice, she had never believed that any man could look at her with such scorn. And yet, how could she have chosen differently? Perhaps, if she had tried to explain to him, she thought now, perhaps if she had told him how sweet Maria was and what a good influence she had upon the Prince, he would have begun to understand and might not have been so ready to censure her.

What was more, Gretna had not been in the Prince's society all these past weeks without realising that he was a very exceptional and brilliant young man. Doubtless there were amongst his friends wild persons who drank too much and gambled too high and who were talked of as being *roués* and depicted in the cartoons as indulging in the most outrageous excesses. But there were also his close friends who were men whose reputations stood high in the State and whose characters and abilities were unquestionable.

Gretna had met Charles Fox and been fascinated by his scintillating wit. She had heard him spar with Richard Brinsley Sheridan at a dinner-table and wished that she could write down every word that they had spoken so as to be able to read it again and learn how words can become a weapon and a delight in the hands of those who know how to use them.

But handsome Mr. Sheridan, with his quick repartee and a severity of temper, had seemed no more brilliant than Mr. Edward Burke, the orator and politician, or, indeed, than Earl Gray or Sir Philip Francis, who had a biting bitterness which seemed to please the Prince when he was more than usually incensed with his father and suffering the frustration that he felt towards all those who censured him in Buckingham House.

Could all these charming and brilliant people be only pretending when they paid court to Maria Fitzherbert? And would the beautiful Duchess of Cumberland and Lady Clairmont and Lady Clare, and all the other people, appear so friendly if they really believed that she was living a life of sin?

It was so impossible to reason it out logically. Maria had said she was to trust her and Gretna was prepared to do that from her very heart.

The following day Harry Carrington arrived in the morning to take her driving in his phaeton in the Park. Gretna, wearing a new coat of blue satin and a little chipstraw bonnet trimmed with blue ribbons to match, ran downstairs to exclaim with delight when she saw the horses he was driving.

"They are magnificent," she cried. "I have never seen finer horseflesh."

"You have seen these before," he answered.

"Have I?" Gretna exclaimed.

"Indeed, yes," he affirmed. "Do you not remember the chestnuts Julien was driving the day we first met? That, indeed, was the reason why I was so keen to purchase them from him."

Gretna drew in her breath. She remembered now—that first moment, as she put her head out of the window of the overturned coach and saw a curricle of yellow and black with a groom at the horses' heads. She could see so clearly the Marquis himself, standing with that cynical smile on his lips watching the stage-coach horses being calmed after he had peremptorily ordered the coachman to their heads.

The Marquis's chestnuts! And he had parted with them to Sir Harry! She wondered why. He was already explaining.

"Julien hates parting with his horses," he said. "But I begged him for these. I told him the very special reason I wanted them was because he was driving them on the day I met you. So he permitted me to buy them—and at not such a fancy price as one might have expected."

"You told him that?" Gretna said.

"But, of course. I drove up to Stade Hall last Saturday. You will remember that was why I could not come to the rout at Cumberland House."

"What was the Marquis doing?" Gretna asked.

"That is precisely what I asked him," Sir Harry said, helping her up into the phaeton and picking up the reins in a manner which showed him to be an accomplished driver and someone she might well be proud to be seen with in the Park.

"And what did he answer?" Gretna prompted.

"He said he was tired of Society. Did you ever hear such fustian?" 'Come back to London,' I said. 'We can't have you mouldering here. Why, you will turn into nothing more or less than a country squire, heavy-booted and turnip-brained. There are at least two new fashions in cravats since you left St. James's.' "

"What was the Marquis's reply?" Gretna questioned.

"He laughed at me. Said he was too old for all our bird-witted junketing. If you ask me, he's still feeling sore about the fair Eloise."

"And who is the fair Eloise?" Gretna asked in a very small voice.

She would not admit even to herself that this was a

question that had been puzzling her for a long time. Sir Harry had the grace to look embarrassed.

"Oughtn't to speak to you of such things," he said abruptly. "Let's talk of something else."

"No, indeed," Gretna protested. "You could not be so disagreeable, having brought the subject up. I am consumed with curiosity. Who is she?"

"Well, if I don't tell you the story, I expect someone else will," Sir Harry replied. "You have heard of the Mistress Eloise Jenkins, haven't you?"

"The actress!" Gretna exclaimed. "Why, we are going to see her at the Drury Lane Playhouse this very evening."

"After you have seen her, perhaps I will tell you the story," Sir Harry said.

"No, no, tell me now," Gretna said. "It will make my visit all the more in . . . interesting."

Sir Harry had to be pressed, but finally it came out. Julien had fallen in love with Mistress Eloise Jenkins when she first appeared in London. It was the fashion at the time for all the smart young men, and especially those who surrounded the Prince, to be in love with play-actresses. The Prince himself was enamoured with Mistress Perdita Robinson, and they all vowed to the object of their affections that their love was eternal and undying.

"To tell the truth, I think Julien only half believed his protestations," Sir Harry said, "but he was convinced that Eloise adored him. She certainly went out of her way to persuade everyone that her heart was deeply engaged."

"How did she do that?" Gretna asked.

"Oh, she paraded about with him as if there was no other man in the world. She even turned down the Prince, so the buzz goes, on one occasion just because Julien asked her to do so. Then when they were drowned in affection, he had to go abroad."

"Why did he have to leave England?" Gretna enquired.

"He was involved in an affair of great moment," Harry Carrington confided. "Nobody knows quite the truth of what happened. But it was whispered that the Prince was challenged to a duel and Julien took his place."

"That would be like him," Gretna said without thinking.

"He's a gamester!" Sir Harry agreed. "And he has always stood up for the Prince. Nobody dares say a word against His Royal Highness in Julien's hearing. Anyway, it was the *on dit* that he deputised for the Prince and killed his man."

"Killed him!" Gretna exclaimed in horror.

"Yes, indeed! And from all reports it was unnecessary to wear the willow. The dead man was an outsider all right. Stands to reason that he must have been if he challenged the Prince to a duel."

"So what happened then?"

"Well, Julien skipped off abroad until the unpleasantness blew over. They say the Prince was extremely grateful to him and did everything he could to smooth things over. But, of course, the relatives of the dead man kicked up a bit of bother."

"Which is hardly surprising," Gretna said.

Sir Harry shrugged his shoulders.

" 'Tis all forgotten now; and if you ask me, Julien could have come back sooner than he did, except maybe he was enjoying himself."

"And what about Mistress Jenkins?" Gretna asked.

"Oh, her! She just ratted on Julien—as, indeed, most ladies of that profession are wont to do when things go wrong."

"Do you mean she would not accompany him?"

"She not only refused to do so, but found another protector within a week of his departure," Sir Harry said.

"How despicable!" Gretna cried indignantly.

"Well, the story is that Julien was extremely hipped by her behaviour. Anyway, she said some low-down things about him and one of Julien's friends made a fine dust-up about it. Not that she cared. Buckmaster is as rich as blazes and has set her up in rare style, I can tell you that."

"Better than the Marquis did?" Gretna asked.

"Oh, better by far, but then Julien never did do her over-proud. That is what makes me think he wasn't so much enamoured as everybody believed. If you ask me, it was his pride that was hurt more than his heart—if Julien has a heart, which I very much doubt."

"Why do you say that?" Gretna enquired.

"He's a cynical chap, isn't he? Told me only on Saturday that love was an idiocy only really believed in by beardless youths and drunken men."

Gretna felt her fingers tighten against each other.

"Did he really say that?" she asked, conscious of a quiver of pain in her heart.

"Oh, he said it right enough with a sneer in his voice and a smile on his lips. I told him there was never such a fellow for trying to cast a damper. But he let me have the horses, which was what I wanted."

There was silence as they rounded Hyde Park Corner and drove into the Park. Then, in a voice which sounded faint and weak even to her own ears, Gretna asked:

"Did . . . he mention . . . me?"

"Now I come to think of it, I don't believe he did," Sir Harry said cheerily. "Well, that shows you can't be too badly in his black books, because, if he disapproved of you, Julien would have told me pretty forcibly not to make a fool of myself where you were concerned. He's done it often enough before."

It was cold comfort, but Gretna tried to make the best of it. They rounded the Park twice and were drawn up in the Row beside the carriage that held Lady Clairmont, who was known to be a close friend of Marie Antoinette and the Duke of Orleans, when another carriage came up beside them.

"And what are you doing with Stade's chestnuts, Harry?" a voice asked silkily.

Gretna turned quickly and then put her hand on Sir Harry's arm.

"Let us go on," she said in a whisper, but he did not hear her.

"I have just bought them," he replied proudly, and Lord Wroxhall, pulling his own pair to a standstill, said approvingly:

"They were worth every penny of what you paid for them, whatever that might be."

"That's what I thought," Sir Harry answered.

"Beautiful horses for a beautiful lady, eh, Harry?" Lord Wroxhall asked, and now his heavy-lidded, hateful eyes were on Gretna.

She wanted to shrink away from him, to hide her face, and then pride made her face him squarely, her chin held high.

"Won't you present me?" Lord Wroxhall asked in his hateful manner, his eyes flickering over her in a way which made her feel as if she stood naked before him.

"But, of course," Sir Harry answered. "I thought you knew each other. Gretna, may I present Lord Wroxhall? Miss Gretna Hayden."

"My Lord!"

Gretna's inclination of the head was imperious and perfunctory. In reply Lord Wroxhall swept his beaver hat from his head, staring at her, as he did so, for a few seconds before he said:

"I think we have, indeed, met before, Miss Hayden."

"I am afraid you are mistaken, my Lord. I have not been long in London and had we met at any of the parties I have enjoyed with my friend, Mistress Fitzherbert, I should remember."

"So, it is you who are staying with Mistress Fitzherbert," Lord Wroxhall said. "I had heard that she had one of her childhood friends with her in St. James's Square."

It was obvious, Gretna thought, that until this moment he had not known where she was staying, though he had recognised her in Sir Harry's phaeton. She said nothing but merely inclined her head and after a moment he asked:

"May I have the honour of calling on you?"

"We are very engaged, my Lord." She turned from him to Sir Harry. "Pray let us drive on. We appear to be holding up the traffic."

It was a snub and Lord Wroxhall knew it. He pulled his horses to the side to let them pass, but as they drove away at a sharp pace the look he gave Gretna was not angry but rather amused.

"Setting him down a peg, weren't you?" Sir Harry asked enquiringly as soon as they were out of earshot.

"He is a bad, evil man," Gretna stormed. "Promise me that you will never leave me alone in his company."

"I promise you that," Sir Harry said. "And I will take good care to leave you alone in nobody's company if I can help it. But what do you know of him?"

"Enough to know that he is wicked," Gretna said. "Do not press me, Harry, for I have no intention of relating to you what I know of Lord Wroxhall. But I dislike him and he frightens me."

She played for a moment with the idea of telling him of Lord Wroxhall's bet to get rid of Maria, and then she thought it sounded too nonsensical. After all, he had been drunk at the time he made it, or, if not drunk, in a state of having had too much liquor, and more than likely he would have forgotten his bet the following morning.

It was quite obvious that he was powerless to hurt Maria or defame her so long as she had the protection of the Prince of Wales and his friends. At the same time,

Gretna did not underestimate Lord Wroxhall. He would be a formidable enemy and, what was more, she felt sure in her heart that he would never forgive her for having made a fool of him in front of the Marquis.

His own servants must have laughed as they carried her trunk higher up the Square; and to have been made a fool of was perhaps the greatest punishment she could have inflicted on him. She had been rude and yet he had smiled. That in itself was sinister and made her feel afraid.

He would have recognised her long before he spoke to Sir Harry. He might, indeed, have seen her on other occasions, although she did not think so. There had undoubtedly been surprise in his eyes when she had told him with whom she was staying.

"Oh, promise to keep him away from me," she cried again, and Sir Harry looked down at her in consternation.

"You are not really afraid of the fellow, are you?" he asked. "I never have liked Wroxhall—and he's got a pretty unsavoury reputation where women are concerned. But he wouldn't dare do anything to upset you. After all, you have only to tell the Prince if he becomes obnoxious."

"Yes, I could do that, couldn't I?" Gretna said, but somehow the words did not soothe her agitation.

She had a sudden longing for the Marquis and almost painfully the memory came back to her of the times he had saved her before. She could feel again the strength of his arm and the security of his shoulder as she had hidden her face against it in the small salon at Stade Hall. She could feel, too, the utter relief that had swept over her when she had seen him alight from his coach in Berkeley Square and had known that she need run no further and there was no question of Lord Wroxhall catching her.

"If only he were here now," she thought, and felt a sudden aching longing for him which swept aside all her pretence and all the efforts she had made to tell herself that she was not in love.

She loved him! She loved him! There was nothing she could do about it, and yet it was hopeless to go on pretending it was not true.

She wanted him. She wanted to know that he was there, to save her and protect her, to awaken that strange, breathless feeling within her that had held them both spellbound on the balcony at Carlton House.

And then she knew, with a sudden dropping of her

heart and with a sense of almost desperate despair, that he had gone for ever. She had seen the scorn and contempt in his face; she had heard the ice on his voice, and knew that he despised her as much as he condemned and despised Maria Fitzherbert, if not indeed more.

They were two of a kind and he had no use for either of them.

9

"YOU LOOK SAD, dearest," Maria remarked as Gretna sighed for perhaps the third time as she stood at the window watching the carriages pass round St. James's Square.

"Oh, but I'm not," Gretna replied with forced gaiety. "How could you think me so ungracious and ungrateful when you are so kind to me and there are so many amusements filling every hour of the day?"

In answer Maria put out her hand and drew Gretna towards her so that they sat side by side on the satin-covered sofa.

"I love having you here," she said softly. "And you are, indeed, the belle of every ball to which I take you. Yet, sometimes I have a suspicion that your heart is heavy and you are not as happy as you appear."

"Oh, but I am, I am," Gretna protested. And yet, even while she lied and was ashamed of telling falsehoods, she knew that she could not tell the truth.

It was impossible to say to someone as sweet, as kind and as gentle as Maria, "I am in love with your enemy, with the man who defames you and who thinks you are just an immoral schemer pretending affection for the Prince for what you can get out of him."

How could the Marquis be so blind? she had asked herself again and again in the silence of the night. How could he believe only the cruel and wicked things that were said about Maria and not see or understand the good influence she had on the Prince? Why did he not see how she managed, in some subtle way of her own, to keep His Royal Highness away from the wilder sparks and dandies who were only too ready to lure him into excesses of drink and gambling?

No, she could not tell Maria her troubles; and she knew, instinctively, that Maria did not confide in her the many difficulties which beset her on every side. She always appeared calm and serene, and yet Gretna knew that she lived, as it were, on the edge of a precipice, torn between her desire to love the Prince as he loved her and her terror that she might hurt or injure him in any way.

Gretna knew, too, that Maria was worried with financial difficulties. Although she had been left a large fortune by Mr. Fitzherbert—people whispered that it was over £2,000 a year—the semi-Royal state which she kept up in St. James's Square must cost double or treble that amount.

Thinking of this now, Gretna said:

"Maria, I must speak to you about my future. I cannot stay on here indefinitely, contributing nothing towards my keep and costing you money for clothes and for all the other things that you give me."

Maria laughed.

"Dearest, do you really think that the infinitesimal amount that you cost could be weighted in comparison with the joy and happiness you give me just by your being here? I have always longed for a sister and I feel that I have found one in you. And, what is more, sometimes I think you are the only friend I can dare . . . trust."

Her voice was lowered at the last words and Gretna put out her hands impulsively.

"You know that you can trust me, Maria. I love you. There is nothing I would not do for you."

"Then stay with me," Maria begged. "Do not talk of going away, but keep me company." She smiled at Gretna and then added: "Indeed, I sometimes think that it does me the world of good to have someone like you as my companion. Even the most slanderous and vicious tongues can find nothing wrong or bad to say in the face of such innocence and such beauty."

"Oh, Maria, when you speak like that you make me feel ashamed and humble," Gretna said. "I am not worthy of such kindness."

"Indeed, you are," Maria retorted. "And do not let us have any more nonsense about earning your living. To tell the truth, dearest, I do not think you would be very good at it."

Gretna laughed a little ruefully.

"I should be hard put to it to know where to start," she admitted. "But I expect I would find someone to employ me."

"Well, you are not going to try," Maria said sternly. "What I want you to do now is to choose with me a pattern from these new materials that have just arrived from France for an evening gown."

"Another one!" Gretna exclaimed.

"Yes, indeed," Maria answered. "The one you wore last night is in ribbons and two others have been ruined by the crush at Crewe House and the rout given by Lady Southampton. But do not let us repine for them. I declare, when you see the new gauzes from Paris, you will be glad they are finished and you have an excuse to replace them."

Maria rose as she spoke and going to her escritoire brought from it a collection of shimmering, gaily coloured patterns which Gretna knew had come from the most expensive shop in Bond Street.

"Maria!" she said impulsively. "Do you ever think how different your life is now? You were so quiet and unfashionable before you were a widow. I remember once your saying that you were not interested in the mode and preferred to be clothed only in the quietest and most subdued colours."

"I remember," Maria answered. "Strange how quickly and easily one changes without really realising that one does so. But the Prince likes me to wear blue, green or white, all of which, he declares, show off my fair hair."

"Golden hair!" Gretna corrected. "I have never seen anyone else with hair that really is like sunshine. It is so beautiful, Maria. You are wise to keep it always unpowdered."

"At least in that I set my own fashion," Maria said a little proudly.

"In others too," Gretna said. "I heard Lady Southampton say the other night that it was impossible not to admire your modesty and the dignity which so many ladies who attend Carlton House try to emulate. She did not know I was listening, but I felt proud that she should speak of you in such a warm manner."

"Did she really say that?" Maria asked, flushing a little. "It is hard always to be dignified, for the Prince loves to be gay and even to indulge in practical jokes. And while I do not wish to seem a prig, I want above all things to remain a lady."

"And that is exactly what you are," Gretna smiled.

"I am so glad you have told me of this," Maria cried. "For a long time I have felt that my actions count for nothing, and that in trying to set a standard I have been laughed at and scorned. Now, quite unexpectedly, you give me praise when I least expected it, and hope!"

"No-one could help admiring you," Gretna said impulsively.

Maria smiled faintly and sighed.

"If that could only be true," she said. "But, alas, there are all too many people who not only disapprove, but say the most slanderous and wicked things about me. Sometimes, Gretna, when I hear what is said or see the cartoons, I wish the Prince and I had never met."

Then, even as she spoke, she gave a little cry.

"No, that is untrue, that is a bad and wicked thing to say, because it denies what is more to me than life itself—my love for him and his love for me."

She spoke passionately and Gretna was transfixed by the intensity of her feelings.

"Oh, Maria," she whispered. "What will be the end of it all?"

It was as if her question was one which Maria had asked herself all too often. She stared at Gretna for a moment with blind eyes and then rose and walked towards the fire-place. For a moment she stood looking at her own reflection. The mirror portrayed faithfully the beauty of her gold hair, her oval face and lovely, vivacious eyes. Then she said very quietly:

"Whatever happens, whatever the future holds, it will have been worth it, worth it because love matters more than anything people can do or say to destroy it."

Her words caused Gretna to feel an almost stabbing ache in her own heart. She loved the Marquis, loved him despite his scorn of her, despite the disdain and what seemed to her in retrospect the disgust that she had seen in his eyes when they last parted.

In that moment she envied her friend as she had never envied her before. She had known the fulfilment of ecstasy and happiness when she and the Prince were alone together and the tempestuous world outside was shut away from them.

She thought again of that moment on the balcony when

the Marquis had looked deep into her eyes and she had felt as if she was caught up into some strange heaven when nothing mattered except that they were joined together by indivisible bonds that were stronger than steel.

And now he hated her! She heard her own voice crying out at it, saw again the icy steel in his eyes and heard his voice almost like a whiplash declaim her for what he believed her to be. She could have cried bitterly at the thought of it.

She felt as if her whole body was bruised and aching because of what he had done to her, but she knew that even if she had to make the choice again she would still be loyal to Maria, still stay where she was rather than betray her friend.

And then the pain of what she had to bear seemed almost too much for her. She felt that she must tell Maria a little of what she was feeling. She must at least speak to her of the Marquis; even to talk of him might be some relief to the agony of her need of him.

"Maria . . ." she began, and then at that moment the door was burst open and the Prince stood there.

His sudden entrance, the wild expression on his face, the manner in which he had arrived, unannounced and unexpected, made both women turn towards him with an exclamation of surprise upon their lips.

He slammed the door behind him, then rushed across the room to Maria, kissing both her hands wildly and then half falling on his knees beside her.

"Maria! Maria! What am I to do?" he cried wildly.

"What has happened? Oh, Sire, what has happened?" Maria asked in dismay. "Come and sit down. Tell me quietly, for I can see you are distraught."

In answer the Prince left Maria's side and walked swiftly up and down the room.

"Quietly! How can I say anything quietly?" he asked. "When I tell you what has happened, the insult, the humiliation of it, then you will understand."

Gretna had heard that the Prince was very emotional on occasions, but she had never imagined that he could be so theatrical or so exaggerated, whatever his feelings.

"I am finished, finished in every possible way!" he cried. "Now there is nothing more I can do, nothing more I can endure. This is too much to be borne by human flesh and blood."

"Sire, you must tell me what has occurred," Maria said

firmly; and Gretna, suddenly realising that she was staring almost open-mouthed at the Prince, made as if to leave the room.

"Stop, Gretna," he said. "Do not go. I want you to hear, too, how I am treated."

"Is it the King?" Maria asked quietly.

"It is, indeed," the Prince replied. "Who else would wish to humiliate me in front of my friends and advisers? Once again I have fallen into the trap. Once again I believed that he would really do something for me."

"Then he has refused to pay your debts?" Maria said, obviously suddenly becoming aware of what all this was about.

"Yes, he has refused!" the Prince answered. "Refused after all this time, after all these negotiations! You know the position I am in. The Jews will advance no more; the money-lenders and the tradesmen are so importunate that if nothing is done at once—at once, I tell you—the bailiffs will enter Carlton House."

"I know all this," Maria said. "But I believed, and I prayed, that Mr. Pitt would succeed in getting at least a portion of the two hundred and fifty thousand pounds Your Royal Highness needs."

"A portion!" the Prince cried. "I am to have nothing, nothing, unless"—he paused—"unless I cease to be a party man and marry."

Maria put her hands up to her face.

"Oh, no, not that," she whispered.

"That is what my father says," the Prince said. "And you know as well as I do why he says it. He hates me. He has always hated me."

He brought his fist down on the mantelshelf so fiercely that the china ornaments seemed likely to leap on to the hearth.

"But I was persuaded as, indeed, Mr. Sheridan and Mr. Fox were persuaded too—that His Majesty would help you this time," Maria said.

"He promised to consider the matter, did he not?" the Prince asked. "I would not have given him a detailed statement of my liabilities unless Mr. Pitt had assured me that he really intended to help me this time."

Maria sighed.

"I am afraid," she said, "that His Majesty asked for a detailed statement just because he wanted to know how and on whom you had spent your money."

"God knows that is true enough!" the Prince answered. "It is all part and parcel of his attempt to set me down and make me appear a dissolute waster. That is what he wants me to be. That is what he does his best to enforce. But I will not tolerate such trickery and double dealing!"

The Prince spoke so violently that Maria laid her hand on his arm.

"Pray, Sire, try to be calm," she pleaded. "No good will come of upsetting yourself in such a manner. Has His Majesty really refused everything, even an increase in your allowance?"

The Prince brought a letter from his pocket.

"See for yourself," he said. "I shall show it to everyone; I shall publish it if necessary. They shall read how inhuman a father can be."

There was silence as Maria read the letter. Then with tears in her eyes she said:

"I am afraid, Sire, that I am to blame in this. I knew when you put down so honestly the sum of fifty-four thousand pounds for the jewellery, plate and furniture that you have given me and spent in this house that His Majesty would be incensed."

"He has made that an excuse," the Prince retorted. "He had no intention of paying up whatever my debts had been. He has always been the same. He has made my life a hell since the day I was born."

"No, Sire, it is my fault," Maria sighed.

"I will not have you blame yourself," the Prince replied.

"If only I had the money to help you," she murmured.

"I have run you into debt as it is," the Prince said. "I am well aware of that, but how can we help it when so many people look to us to lead Society, to make London a place of gaiety rather than a morgue such as can be found at Buckingham House."

"What will you do?" Maria asked despairingly.

"Heaven alone knows," the Prince answered, and then looked across the room at Gretna. "I am glad you have heard this, little Gretna," he said. "Now you see what unhappiness, cruelty and hardness of heart can be inflicted by those who do not love their children."

"But, Sire, what can you do?" Gretna asked, aghast at the proportion of the sums of money to which she had just listened.

She knew a great deal about poverty, for her father and mother had been poor all their lives, desperately poor. She had seen them afraid when the bills came in, she had seen them worried and anxious as to where the next penny was to come from. But the Prince's debts were to her even more terrifying because of their magnitude.

Two hundred and fifty thousand pounds! With the half-year just past there would be bills pouring in and other claims falling due.

"What can I do?" the Prince asked, and it seemed to her that he asked it directly of her.

"There is only one thing that can be done, Sire," she replied. "You must economise."

The Prince, who had sunk down despondently in a chair after the last question, sprang to his feet.

"But of course!" he cried. "Why did I not think of it before? We must economise, Maria, but drastically, dramatically, publicly."

"What can you mean, Sire?" Maria asked anxiously.

"I have thought of something," the Prince said in a very different voice from that in which he had been declaiming so wildly the moment before. "It will be sensational, it will be worth it to see my father's face. I will call his bluff—if bluff it is. And if not, then I will carry out my threats to the very letter."

"You must tell me, Sire, what you intend to do," Maria pleaded unhappily.

To Gretna's astonishment the Prince, where he had been in the utter depths of despondency, now seemed quite gay. She had realised before that he was always in extremes; and now that he was resolved upon a certain step it was quite obvious that nothing anyone could say would stop him.

"I want writing-paper and a quill," he said.

"Pray, do not do anything rash," Maria begged. "Let me send for Mr. Fox and Mr. Sheridan. Let us at least consult with them before you take any decisive step."

"I have made up my mind," the Prince said airily. "I have been crushed and put upon long enough. I am a man, not a frightened boy to stand trembling in case I do not receive my week's pocket-money. No, His Majesty shall have a reply. The reply of a man who will stand no more of this infamous and unreasonable treatment."

"Oh, please, Sire, please!" Maria begged.

She put her hand on his arm as he walked towards the writing-table. He picked up the quill and raised it to his lips. "Marriage, Maria! That was the condition," he said. "Marriage! We both know the answer to that command."

"Sire! Sire! You must be subtle, you must be clever over this, you must not do anything rash."

"I shall do what should have been done before," the Prince said. "I will send my father an ultimatum that either he pays my debts or I will take steps immediately to economise in a manner such as neither he nor his pie-faced advisers have ever imagined possible."

"But, how can you do that, Sire!" Gretna asked.

It was presumptuous of her to ask the question and yet she could not help it bursting from her lips.

The Prince looked across the room at her with a faint smile on his lips.

"I shall do just what you suggested," he said. "I shall shut up Carlton House, sell my horses and reduce every expense in my household, even those necessary to my birth and rank, until I have totally liberated myself from my present embarrassments."

"But, Sire, you cannot do such a thing," Gretna protested.

"It is what you suggested," the Prince said. "My horses shall be paraded through the streets to Tattersalls; the workmen who are still employed on the unfinished wing of Carlton House shall be dismissed, but the scaffolding shall remain as a witness to the straits to which the Heir Apparent to the Throne of England is reduced."

"But, Sire, I never suggested such a thing!" Gretna cried.

The Prince was not listening to her. He was reciting what he would do with almost relish, as if he could see all too clearly the King's embarrassment.

"I shall shut my stables; the horses' liveries and harnesses must be sold by public auction. Those servants who wish to remain at Carlton House must do so on reduced wages."

"Where will you go?" Maria asked, through lips which seemed suddenly white. "Where will you stay?"

The Prince looked round the room as if for inspiration, and then he suddenly clapped his hands together.

"We will go to Brighthelmstone," he said. "But, of course! That is where we will go, Maria. And, what is more, I shall travel there in a hired post-chaise. That will show the King, if nothing else does, that I mean what I say."

"In a hired post-chaise!" Maria repeated faintly.

"That is what I have said," the Prince said, "and that is what I will do. And you and Gretna will do the same. Close this house, Maria. Tell Lord Uxbridge you have no further need of it. Send back any of the plate and furniture for which you can obtain a good price."

"If that is your wish. I will do it," Maria said in a low voice.

"And now for my letter," the Prince said, turning to the writing-table. "And while I am writing it send a flunkey for Richard Sheridan. If he cannot write a play out of this drama then I declare he is not the playwright I believe him to be. What a plot, do you not agree, Maria? I might even persuade Sheridan to call it "Another School for Scandal." For that is what this will be—a scandal that will shock Britain."

The Prince stopped suddenly just as he was about to pick up the quill. Maria was in tears, and as he saw them filling her eyes and running down her soft cheeks he sprang forward and put his arms round her.

"Maria, my darling angel! I would not have you cry," he said. "My cursed debts are not worth one tear from your sweet, loyal heart."

His lips sought hers and Gretna slipped from the room, closing the door softly behind her. For a moment she stood outside, her head in a whirl, hardly being able to believe that what she had seen and heard had taken place in all reality and had not been just a figment of her imagination.

But a few hours later she learned the Prince's letter had gone to Buckingham House and that Maria was wholeheartedly supporting him in his campaign of economy.

For the next two or three days they were almost unbelievably busy. There was so much to be packed up in the house, so many letters to be written, so many explanations to be made. Almost every other hour, it seemed to Gretna, the Prince was hurrying in and out, saying what he had done, enjoying—it was quite obvious—every moment of the drama in which he was playing the lead.

He was more than delighted when he learned that many people were saying that the King spent too much money on the Queen's needy German relatives and a cartoon was being sold on the streets depicting the King and Queen coming out of the Treasury loaded with money-bags and the Prince following in the rags of the prodigal son.

But what pleased the Prince more than anything was the fact that in getting away from London he was going to Brighthelmstone. He talked of it incessantly, and when, two or three days after the Prince and his small suite had left, Gretna drove down with Maria as the Prince had done by hired post-chaise, she could understand his enthusiasm.

But before they left she had an encounter that had left her frightened and fearful. Maria had gone over to Carlton House to advise the Prince on what pictures he should sell and what should be retained. Gretna was alone in St. James's Square when the butler suddenly announced Lord Wroxhall.

She sprang to her feet and faced him as he crossed the drawing-room, looking, she thought, more odious and more sinister than usual. He wore a many-caped riding-coat and it was obvious from the rest of his attire that he had been travelling.

"What do you want, my Lord?" Gretna asked coldly.

"You were not expecting me?" he said in surprise, glancing around the room to see if she was, indeed, alone.

"I know no reason why my hostess, Mistress Fitzherbert, should expect you to visit this house, my Lord," Gretna replied.

"Then she cannot have confided in you, my dear," he answered.

"I do not know what you mean," Gretna said.

He stood looking at her as she had not invited him to be seated, and then suddenly took a step forward which made her shrink instinctively away from him.

"If you come any nearer," she warned, "I shall ring the bell for the servants."

"You are entrancing when you are angry," he said. "How many moods you affect so gracefully, how fortunate the man who watches them and who has the privilege of producing them at will!"

"I am not interested in your compliments, my Lord."

She felt the sudden frustration and fear that nothing she said really had any effect on him. He just watched her, his evil, bloodshot eyes seeming to devour her face, her frightened eyes, the agitation of her breasts, the pulse beating nervously at the base of her white throat. He took it all in and she knew she aroused everything that was base and bestial in his nature.

"You are safe enough . . . for the moment," he said

slowly. There was a pause before the last three words. "Today I do business for my Prince. Tomorrow, who knows? I may be a free man and ready to pursue you."

"If you have business with His Royal Highness, then you will not find him here." Gretna said, holding herself stiffly. "He is, I believe, at Carlton House."

"Doubtless with the fair Maria in attendance!" Lord Wroxhall said sneeringly.

"Do not dare speak of Mistress Fitzherbert in such a manner," Gretna cried angrily, and added: "Would your Lordship oblige me by leaving?"

"So fiery, so sweet. What pleasure to kiss those lips until they cry for mercy," Lord Wroxhall retorted. "I told you the first time that I saw you that you were unbroken. I thought the noble Marquis was the one to do that. I was mistaken. I shall reserve that infinite pleasure for myself."

"Will you go away or must I have you thrown out?" Gretna asked, her hand raised towards the bell-pull.

Lord Wroxhall bowed.

"I will leave," he said. "But if I am unfortunate enough not to find Mistress Fitzherbert at Carlton House, will you be gracious enough to inform her that a villa has been found for her at Brighthelmstone—a modest, pretty little place with green shutters, separated from the Pavilion, where His Royal Highness will be staying, by only a strip of garden."

Lord Wroxhall somehow contrived to make his description sound insulting. Without saying a word in answer Gretna merely rang the bell.

"The footman will be waiting to show you out, my Lord," she said, and turned her back to him, walking across the room to stare blindly out of the window, conscious, to her own annoyance, that her hands were trembling visibly.

"We shall meet at Brighthelmstone, my dear," Lord Wroxhall said softly, then she heard him go and the door closed behind him, but his hateful presence seemed to linger on in the Salon even after she knew he had left the house.

She was to learn, when Maria returned, that he had, indeed, been given the task, by the Prince, of finding a house in which she could stay in Brighthelmstone.

"You know, dearest," Maria explained, "I cannot stay under the same roof as the Prince. He has asked me to do so, but I said firmly that we would not join him in Brighthelmstone until a house could be found for me."

"It appears that Lord Wroxhall has procured one," Gretna said, not liking to say how much she loathed and detested the man or, indeed, to relate to Maria the wager that she had heard him make when she was at Carlton House.

He would have forgotten about it now, she thought, and there was no need to upset Maria. In fact she had long learned never to repeat to her friend anything that was unkind or unpleasant. Maria had enough to suffer without that.

"So now we can go to Brighthelmstone," Maria said gaily. "I am grateful, indeed, to Lord Wroxhall for finding us a house. The Prince has delayed his departure just because he did not wish to leave me. Now he can go ahead and somehow I think we will be very happy there."

"You have been there before?" Gretna asked.

"Yes, two years ago," Maria answered. "In fact, soon after the Prince first discovered the village and decided to build a house there on the site of the one where he stayed at that time."

"I am longing to see it," Gretna said.

"And so am I," Maria admitted. "We shall all enjoy the sea air while the Prince swears that the sea-bathing does more good to the glands in his throat, which sometimes distress him by swelling, than anything else he has ever tried. Oh, Gretna, what fun it is going to be after all!"

She was like a young girl, Gretna thought, and putting her arms around Maria, she kised her tenderly.

They chattered gaily in the hired post-chaise all down the long Brighthelmstone road until finally the Downs came in sight and then, at last, the charming village which, even with its Royal patronage, had only just emerged from the obscurity of a fishing hamlet.

Gretna only had a moment, as they drew up with a flourish at a little house with green shutters, to take in the beauties of the Marine Pavilion with its big, circular dome and Ionic columns which connected it to two other wings. Then they hurried into the little villa and found, as Maria must have expected, that the Prince was awaiting her there.

He ran forward as eagerly as a boy to take her hands, to draw her up into the pretty little drawing-room with its balconies looking out towards the sea.

"You have come! You have come!" he said excitedly. "I have hardly been able to content myself without you, Maria. I want you to see the Pavilion at once, to approve all that I have done. You will be astonished."

"I am sure I shall, Sire," Maria answered, looking happily into his eyes. "Give me just a few moments to wash my hands and change my gown and then I will come with you at once."

She hurried from the room as eager as a schoolgirl at an expected treat, and the Prince turned to Gretna.

"I thought we had left the Season behind," he said, "but quite a lot of our friends are pouring into the town, determined to show their loyalty. And many of your friends are here too."

"My friends, Sire?" Gretna asked in surprise.

"One in particular, shall I say? Who says that he admires you exceedingly. He has asked me to further his suit by asking you to look on him kindly."

"And who can that be, Sire?" Gretna asked a little apprehensively.

She knew what was coming and felt herself already begin to tremble, and yet even so the name came like a blow.

"Who but my good friend Lord Wroxhall?" the Prince asked smilingly.

10

THE NEXT FEW days the sun was shining and Brighthelmstone seemed to Gretna a place of enchantment. In front of the Pavilion was a lawn filled with shrubs and flowers, and beyond that, going down to the sea, was a broad open space which was known as the Stein.

Every day the Prince and Maria walked along the Stein, taking in the sea air and meeting their friends and acquaintances. It was all very informal; and still more unconventional were the gay little dinner-parties which took place either in the Pavilion or at Maria's house.

Gretna found these far more amusing and entertaining than the great throngs at Carlton House had ever been.

Only the Prince's closest and quieter friends had followed him to Brighthelmstone. The rowdy, wild young sparks had stayed in London, unable to tear themselves away from the gambling hells and the clubs. Gretna was sure the Prince did not miss them and certainly Maria seemed happier than she had ever been.

The strict economy which had seemed so frightening at first now made it easy for her to persuade the Prince not to give the huge dinner-parties or packed receptions which he had believed were such an essential part of his life.

"We are just a little family party, Sire. Is not that more fun?" Maria asked one evening after dinner when there had been eight of them round the polished silver-laden table and the conversation had been so witty and gay that Gretna had laughed and laughed and for a time had forgotten the ache in her heart.

"You know that I like it above all things," the Prince answered, and taking Maria's hand kissed it.

There had been complete sincerity in his voice and Gretna really believed that he had no regrets for the glories that had passed.

The following morning he came to Maria's house to tell her, rather sourly, how little he had gained by the sale of his horses, the pictures and all the other things that had been put up for public auction.

"A paltry seven thousand!" he related. "It is hardly enough to justify an abusive letter from my father accusing me of being undignified, theatrical and revengeful."

"Try not to let it hurt you, Sire," Maria begged. "Your true friends know, as I do, that you have a real and honourable desire to pay your just debts. That is enough. Let us forget the unkind things which would be said whatever you did."

"That is true enough," the Prince agreed. "He hates me! You know he hates me!"

"But the people are proud of what you are doing," Maria answered, and she showed him some of the newspapers which had come from London and which praised the Prince in no uncertain manner.

Nevertheless, however happy he might be at Brighthelmstone, it was obvious that the Prince still smarted under his father's attacks and hoped, almost against hope, that the King would relent.

He seemed to cling to Maria in those moments and at

such times she became more like a mother to him than a lover, consoling and comforting him and raising his spirits when they sank into the depths of depression.

It was then that Gretna felt a little in the way and effaced herself as cleverly as she could without being obvious about it. It was not so easy in such a tiny house and she was undisguisedly glad when Sir Harry appeared unexpectedly one afternoon when they were walking on the Stein.

"Sir Harry!" she exclaimed, her eyes dancing. "I had no suspicion that you were coming to Brighthelmstone."

"Then you must be bird-witted," he teased her. "You know full well I would follow you to Hell if you led me there."

She laughed at that, but her eyes fell before his because there was no disguise about the affection he felt for her. When he had greeted Maria and the Prince, they fell a little behind so that they could talk without being overheard.

"How is the Prince bearing up?" Sir Harry asked in a low voice.

"Wonderfully," Gretna replied. "I think he is almost enjoying his economies. Maria makes him count every penny that he spends and they have quite a game trying to remember each paltry expenditure."

"I told Julien everything would be all right," Sir Harry remarked. "But he has been worrying after the Prince all the way down here, like an old hen with only one chick."

"Is the Marquis here?" Gretna asked.

She managed to speak lightly, but her heart turned over in her breast and she felt suddenly agitated, her hands instinctively flying towards the tumult in her heart.

"Yes, indeed," Sir Harry answered. "We are both here, and fine and dandy in a slap-up house Julien has taken right on the Marine Parade."

"I . . . I should have thought such a small place would have . . . bored his Lordship," Gretna faltered.

"I don't think it will," Sir Harry answered seriously. "But you never know with Julien. He's a funny fellow. He takes the strangest fancies, and then, when one least expects it, gets as mad as fire in a quiet, deep way which shrivels a man up."

"Has something incensed him at the moment?" Gretna could not help asking.

"No, I don't think so," Sir Harry replied, but she had the idea that he was lying.

They had walked quite a long way and the Prince and Maria turned back. As they did so, Sir Harry exclaimed:

"Look! There's Julien, driving his new greys. Did you ever see such a pair? I am green with envy, as, indeed, I have told him."

Gretna looked and felt as if the very ardency of her glance must draw the Marquis's attention to them. And yet he seemed not to see them, but drove past at a spanking pace, the sunshine glittering on the silver embellishments of his curricle, the tiger at the back grinning back impudently as if he was well aware that the turn-out was smarter than anything else to be seen on the Parade.

"Demme! What's he do to make everyone else seem down-at-heel?" Sir Harry asked with a wry-grin, and Gretna thought it was because the Marquis himself was so distinguished.

It was not merely the rakish set of his beaver hat or the cut of his coat, which fitted with never a wrinkle, or the polish on his boots, which she had learned from one of the dandies was due to champagne. There was, in addition, an indefinable quality about him which made him seem superior to other men, and yet it was something one could never define in words.

"It looks as if we are going to be smart down here," Sir Harry smiled. "The Duke of Queensberry arrives tomorrow and I hear that Sheridan is already here."

"Oh, yes, he arrived the day after we did," Gretna said.

"Well, we certainly shan't be at a loss for entertainment with Eloise Jenkins giving a performance at the theatre."

"Whom did you say?"

Gretna could not help her voice rising a little.

"Eloise Jenkins, the play-actress. It may be a hum, but I was told that she is to appear tomorrow night."

Gretna felt her spirits drop and a sudden black depression settle on her. This, then, was the explanation why the Marquis had come to Brighthelmstone. She knew then the pain of jealousy, the agony of feeling frustrated and forgotten, of wanting a man who desired another woman.

"I am a fool to mind," she told herself, and almost said the words out loud.

"I say, you look pale," Sir Harry said suddenly. "You are not going to have a fit of the vapours or something?"

"No, indeed," Gretna managed to say, and forced a smile to her lips.

"It is all this walking," Sir Harry went on solicitously. "I never did take to it myself. The sooner the Prince goes back to the horseflesh the better for all of us."

Gretna managed to laugh, but all the way back along the Stein she was thinking of only one thing—the Marquis and Eloise. Eloise, whose name she had heard that very first night at Stade Hall. Eloise Jenkins, who had bewitched London with her casting in Mr. Sheridan's plays, whose entrancing smile and graceful manner had seemed to Gretna beyond compare the only time she had seen her at the theatre.

She had felt then that she could understand why the Marquis had fallen for anyone so lovely, so talented and so graceful. But she had believed—as, indeed, she had heard so often—that Mistress Jenkins had transferred her attentions to Lord Buckhurst.

Supposing now she desired the Marquis again? Gretna clenched her fingers together. She felt that she could hardly bear it. To know that the Marquis was angry with her was one thing. To believe that he no longer cared or that he was indifferent to her was infinitely more painful to bear.

They arrived back at Maria's house and the Prince and Sir Harry both stayed for a dish of tea and then made their adieux.

"We will not dine with you tonight, Sire," Maria said as the Prince kissed her hand. "I have a slight headache and I am feared it may turn into a cold. I will go to bed early. It'll be wisest, I am sure of it."

"You must do as you wish," the Prince replied. "But it will be a long evening without you! You know that, Maria, don't you?"

"Nonsense, Sire," she said, smiling into his eyes. You know that you have some very agreeable company this evening. You will not miss me in the slightest."

"I always miss you," he replied, "every moment, every second that you are not there."

Gretna saw his fingers tighten on Maria's hand. For a long moment they looked at each other and then the Prince made one of his beautiful bows, which were the model for all the young beaux, and left the room.

"Is your head bad?" Gretna asked.

"It is, indeed," Maria answered. "I cannot think why, unless I am indeed starting a cold. I pray that is not so.

The Prince fidgets when I have an ailment, however slight."

"Then retire to bed at once," Gretna said. "I will order your dinner on a tray. What would you fancy?"

"You must have yours beside me," Maria said. "Choose what you wish, dearest. I am nöt in the least hungry."

That was obviously true. When the dinner was brought up to her bedchamber, Maria took a few mouthfuls of chicken soup and then set down her spoon and swore she could eat no more. There were dark lines under her eyes and Gretna quickly finished her own meal and had the trays taken from the room.

"I will settle you down," she said. "And then you must go to sleep at once."

"If I am to do that," Maria said with her hand to her forehead. "I think I had best take a little laudanum. My head throbs so dreadfully I am afraid I shall not sleep because of the pain."

"Then it will be a good idea," Gretna agreed. "Where do you keep it?"

"I think you will find some in the cupboard by the washing-stand," Maria answered; and when Gretna looked, she found a small bottle, duly inscribed with the right dosage and with many instructions that it should not be exceeded under any circumstances.

"I think I should be afraid to take this stuff," she said, after reading what was written on the bottle.

"It does not hurt in very small quantities," Marie replied. "And often a deep sleep is a better cure than anything else. Give me the spoon, dearest. It is nasty, but if I swallow it quickly I shan't notice the taste."

Gretna gave it to her, then replaced the bottle in the cupboard, smoothed Maria's pillows and kissed her cheek.

"You look so lovely with your golden hair loose around you," she said admiringly.

"Unfortunately I feel ugly," Maria said with a little smile. She closed her eyes, and Gretna, after arranging the blinds so that they would not rattle in the breeze coming in from the sea, tiptoed out of the room.

She went down to the drawing-room and picked up the embroidery which Maria had persuaded her to start. It was to cover a small footstool, but Gretna had so far not done more than a few inches. She tried to concentrate on it, but her thoughts kept going back to the Marquis.

If she shut her eyes, she could see him so vividly driving

along the Parade. She could see him, too, staring at her that first night at Stade Hall, when she had sat at his feet and something lovely and exciting had passed between them. She had not understood then what it was, but now she knew it was the awakening of her love for him.

There was a sudden knock at the door and one of the maids stood there.

"Excuse me, Miss, but there is a woman downstairs who says the mistress told her to call this evening."

"Oh, but I know who it is!" Gretna exclaimed. "It is the mother of the little boy who was begging from us this afternoon. Mistress Fitzherbert spoke to him; and when she found he was one of six children, she told him to send his mother here this evening and she would have something to give them."

"Shall I tell the mistress the woman is here?" the maid asked.

"Not on any account!" Gretna exclaimed. "She is asleep and must not be disturbed. I know where the things are. We got them ready and Cook was asked to bake a rabbit pie."

"Shall I enquire if she has done so?" the maid asked.

"Yes, do," Gretna said. "And I will speak with the woman and explain why Mistress Fitzherbert cannot see her."

She ran downstairs to the little hall. The woman was standing there, her face worn and lined in the light of the candles. She had an old shawl thrown over her head and the hands that clasped it were work-worn and trembling a little as if from cold.

"Come and sit down," Gretna said kindly, indicating a cushioned settle just inside the door.

"Are you, Ma'am, the lady as I was to see?" the woman asked.

"No, indeed," Gretna replied. "The lady you have come to see is Mistress Fitzherbert. I am only a friend of hers. She was sorry for your little boy this afternoon when he begged of her and His Royal Highness. He told her that you have five other children. Is that right?"

"Yes, lady, and my husband is unable to find work, try as he may."

"I am so sorry," Gretna said simply. "And so is Mistress Fitzherbert. She has got together a few clothes for you and Cook has baked you a rabbit pie."

"Blessings on you, lady," the woman said. "It is good

for the likes of us that the gentry should come to Brighthelmstone. Maybe there will be work of some sort for my husband."

"I am sure there will be——" Gretna began, when she was interrupted by a light knock at the door.

Without thinking, forgetting that she was not at home where it was quite usual for her and her mother to answer the door, she pulled it open. A servant in the Royal livery of scarlet and gold stood there.

"I have a message for Mistress Fitzherbert," he said, in what Gretna felt a somewhat imperious manner.

"I am sorry," Gretna said. "Mistress Fitzherbert cannot be disturbed."

" 'Tis of importance," the man argued.

"Perhaps you will give it to me," Gretna suggested.

"His Royal Highness's compliments and he wishes to see Mistress Fitzherbert immediately. He has sent a carriage to convey her to the Pavilion."

"But . . . I do not think that is possible," Gretna said.

" 'Tis urgent. That's what I was told," the man persisted.

"Wait a moment," Gretna answered.

She shut the door and stood irresolute in the hall. If the Prince had sent for Maria that meant that something unexpected had happened—an order from the King; more trouble about his debts; a communication from the Prime Minister? It might be any of these things. She well knew that the Prince would want Maria's advice. What was more, if she was not there he might be inclined to do something hasty that was foolish and would do harm to his cause.

She ran upstairs and; when she reached the landing outside Maria's bedchamber, knocked very softly on the door. There was, as she expected, no answer, and turning the handle she went in. The room was in darkness. She groped her way to the dresing-table and lit one of the candles.

Maria was sleeping and breathing deeply. It was obvious that the laudanum had taken effect. Gretna hesitated for a moment then called her name.

"Maria! Maria!"

There was no reply. Maria just went on breathing evenly and deeply. Gretna touched her shoulder. It was soft and warm, but there was no response, not even a flicker of the long eyelashes which swept Maria's pale cheeks.

"I shall never waken her," Gretna thought desperately, "and even if I do she will be in no state to go to the Pavilion."

There was only one thing to be done, she thought, and that was to write a letter to the Prince, explaining what had happened and begging him to excuse Maria from attending him, however important it might be.

Leaving the candle burning in case Maria did awake before she had to send the letter, Gretna went downstairs to the drawing-room.

It was only when she reached the elegant writing-desk with its inlaid, cut and embossed legs, that she remembered that only that morning Maria had exclaimed in vexation that the writing-paper had not yet come from the stationers. They had ordered some to be embossed with the name of the villa the very day they had arrived, choosing pale grey paper of superfine texture which Gretna had thought was exceedingly elegant.

No writing-paper! What was she to do? She looked hopefully in the little pigeon-holes of the desk and even opened one or two of the drawers, but while there were seals, sand, wafers and long quills, there was not a sign of a piece of paper.

It was then that Gretna remembered the box that Maria had always kept in her bedchamber. It was quite a large one of polished wood with her initials on it in gold, and Maria had said more than once that it contained all her papers and was of the greatest importance. It had, in fact, travelled down with them in the post-chaise while the rest of the baggage had gone with the servants.

Perhaps there was something in the box on which she could write, Gretna thought, and she sped upstairs again. Maria had not changed her position. Gretna could see that at a glance, and taking the candle in her hand she moved it on to the table by the window where she could see Maria's box had been put.

She half expected to find it locked, but the key was in the lock. She remembered then that Maria had been putting something away just before she got into bed. Gretna opened the lid. The box was filled with papers, letters and what looked to Gretna like deeds.

Feeling that it was an impertinence to do so and yet conscious that the Prince was waiting, she lifted one or two of the top papers, hoping to see a piece of writing-paper. It would not matter what was the address on it, she thought. She could cross that out. It was just that she must have something on which to write her message to the Prince.

It was then she saw, lying in the centre of the box, a large, thick piece of paper. It was the size of a certificate and only after she had looked at it for a second did she realise that quite unconsciously she had read it and realised what it meant. Because she could not help herself, she read it again:

We, the undersigned, do witness yt George Augustus Frederick, Prince of Wales, was married unto Maria Fitzherbert, this 15th day of December 1785.

John Smythe
Henry Errington
George P.
Maria Fitzherbert.

Gretna felt the tears suddenly come into her eyes. It was true then, true what she had always wanted to believe, what she had always known in her heart! Maria was married to the Prince. It seemed impossible, incredible, and yet she had always known that Maria would do nothing that was wrong, nothing that was wicked.

Gretna thought now how often she had tried not to hear, not to think of what went on at St. James's Square when the guests had gone and when she herself had gone to bed. She had tried not to notice the carriage with the drawn blinds which stood outside, not to hear soft footsteps on the stairs just before dawn.

Maria had asked for her trust and she had given it freely. She knew then that always she must fight against the encroaching knowledge which she could not help acquiring because she was a member of the household.

They were married! They were married!

She wanted to cry the words aloud, to take the certificate in her hand, to rush outside the house and proclaim it to the whole world. This would confound those who had sneered and insulted Maria; this would humiliate those who had drawn their skirts aside as if she was too vulgar for them to associate with.

They were married, and the Marquis had said it was impossible. She felt the triumph and the wonder of it fill her whole mind and knew that a burden had fallen from her shoulders.

And then she remembered what the Marquis had said at Stade Hall. Parliament would not stand for it; the country would not stand for it. By marrying Maria the Prince would forfeit his succession!

Gretna felt a little of her triumph ebb away from her. How often she had remembered that no Roman Catholic might marry a member of the Church of England and had tried to make it an excuse for Maria and the Prince.

Now she knew why Maria had kept silent despite the insults, despite the insinuations that were made wherever she went. Now she knew why, when the cartoons and lampoons depicting her in a vile manner were shown to Maria, she had put them gently in the fire and refused even to look at them.

Maria knew in her heart she was married. She knew before the eyes of God she was married. What did it matter what lesser people thought?

Very carefully Gretna covered up the certificate with the letters and closing the box locked it. She knew that she would never speak of this to Maria, she knew that she would never tell anyone what she had seen. This was a secret which must never be revealed, which no-one else should ever know.

And quite suddenly she knew that she admired the Prince more than she had ever admired him before. Maria had taken a risk because of her love. His risk had been infinitely greater. By one action, by a defiance of all the rules and laws of the Realm, he had risked everything for his love and his devotion to one woman.

In that moment she saw him not as an irresponsible, impetuous, passionate young man, but as a knight who was prepared to chance what might be far worse than death in the pursuit of his ideal.

Gretna blew out the candle and tip-toed from the room. Outside on the landing she put her hands to her face and tried to think what she must do, tried to remember that the Prince was waiting for Maria, the carriage was outside, a flunkey on the doorstep.

It was hard for the moment to return to the more mundane and ordinary things, having discovered inadvertently one of the most sensational and world-shaking of them all. Then she remembered that she must steel herself to behaving as if nothing had happened and she knew then that the best thing she could do would be to go to the Prince and explain that Maria was asleep and she could not waken her.

On the landing was a wardrobe. She opened it, looking for a cape of some sort. The first one she saw was one of blue velvet edged with fur, which Maria often wore and which covered her dress completely. It was a little long for Gretna but she put it on, thinking it would save time rather than that she should run up another flight of stairs to where her bedroom was situated, to procure a cloak of her own.

She hurried down the stairs, remembering only when she reached the hall that she had not brought the things Maria had laid aside in the sewing-room for the poor woman. There was not time now to go back. The Prince would be waiting and wondering what had happened. He was quite capable, Gretna thought, of coming over himself if he thought anything was amiss.

She turned to the woman sitting waiting patiently on the settle.

"There is a message that I have got to give to His Royal Highness," she said. "Would you be kind enough to wait until I return? I will not be long, I promise you."

"I don't mind, lady," the woman answered. " 'Tis warm here and peaceful. And peace is something I get little enough of, I can tell you."

"You shall have the things the moment I return," Gretna said. "I am sure I won't be more than ten minutes."

As she opened the front door a guest of wind and rain came bursting over her in a sudden flurry. She pulled the cloak around her, glad that the hood, with its warm fur, protected her hair from the damp. She slammed the door and hurried down the little path. She could see the coach waiting, the candle lanterns flickering in the force of the wind.

The door was opened for her. She stepped forward and as she did so something thick, heavy and enveloping was thrown over her head, stifling her, blinding her, making it, in her confusion, almost impossible to cry out or to struggle.

She felt someone lift her and throw her back against the seat; she heard a hoarse voice give an order; she was jerked backwards as the horses started off. The coach began to move. She tried to struggle, to fight for the freedom of her hands, and then to scream. Almost immediately a heavy hand was placed roughly on her face.

"Open yer bone-box," a coarse voice threatened, "and yer'll get a knock in yer phyz."

11

GRETNA FELT FAINT. The blanket which covered her was thick and suffocating. She felt it grow increasingly difficult to get her breath; what was more, her hands were pinioned and she could only move them a little with a great effort.

She ceased to struggle and lay in the corner of the coach fighting against the feeling of suffocation and nausea which came partly from the smell of the blanket and partly from a fear such as she had never experienced in the whole of her life before.

After a while one of the men spoke.

"Th' fancy mort ain't much of a gabster, Joe," he remarked. "Do yer think her's dead mutton?"

"Maybe ye gave her too much of a lick," was the reply.

"Me!" The man's voice rose a little. "Oi've told ye 'afore, I don't mind handling some cove, but it's not my fancy to muck about with females."

"Ye'll do as ye've bid," was the answer. "Ye'll get a couple o' jacks for th' job an' for that ye can keep yer bone-box shut."

The first man, who had been apprehensive, seemed silenced by this. Gretna felt her faintness lighten and her brain began to work. So the men were being paid for it. Paid for what? That was the question she began to ask herself.

"If her's a-goner," the first man said suddenly in a quavering voice, "that'll be murder, Joe, and Oi don't 'old with murder, not to please any well-breeched swell."

"Aw, stop a-frightening yerself," Joe answered roughly. "Oi oughtn't ter have brought ye on the job. If ye hadn't looked pretty enough ter act th' footman, it'd have been Bill aside me now and none of yer bleating. Stow it. Her's quiet and that's all that we need worrit about. Some of 'em would have been a-squealing like a pricked pig."

"Oi don't like it," the frightened man said plaintively. "'Tis a queer rig and no mistake."

"Shut yer trap," Joe shouted. "If the mort ain't a-goner, her'll know enough to string ye up. Not that her'll be coming back from where we're a-taking her."

"Where be her going?" the timid man asked.

"If Oi knew, Oi wouldn't tell; and as I don't, I needn't shoot the cat. Ye keep her mummer shut 'til we gets to the boat."

There was silence after this except for the clatter of the horses' hooves on the road and the rumble of the wheels. Gretna lay very still. She had no desire for Joe to think she had overheard anything that was said, and she knew only too well from the rough way she had been handled when they put her into the coach that they could easily silence her in a manner which would ensure their safety for evermore.

Why had they kidnapped her? For what reason? And then gradually, out of the horror and chaos of her brain, she began to understand what had happened.

It was Maria they had come to fetch; Maria whom they thought they were kidnapping, not her. As she realised this, she wondered how she could have been so dense for one moment to imagine that anyone would have been interested in her.

Now it was so clear. The footman in the Royal livery who she had thought was rather strange in his manner. The urgent message from the Prince and the carriage waiting outside. Fool! Fool that she had been for one moment to think that the Prince would have sent such a message! His Royal Highness was always so punctilious and courteous in his manner to everybody, most of all to Maria. Had he really required her presence he would have written her a note. He would never for one moment have thought of sending her a message by a servant.

Gretna could have cried aloud at her own stupidity. How could she have been so blind, so idiotic not to have sensed that something was wrong, something was strange in the message and in the flunkey's behaviour?

If Maria had been awake she felt she might have been suspicious at once. And yet would she have been? How could she imagine for one moment that anyone would have concocted such a dastardly, such a fantastic plot as that of kidnapping her?

And yet if Gretna had not decided to go to the Prince with an explanation, if there had been writing-paper in the villa—so many other ifs and buts—Maria would be in her place now, trussed up and helpless, being carried through the night by two illiterate and murderous-minded men who were in the pay of someone else.

No need to ask who that someone else might be. Gretna knew the answer to that almost before the question formulated itself in her mind. Had she not heard with her own ears Lord Wroxhall swear in the Salon in Carlton House that he would be rid of Maria within three months? This was his plot, she was sure of it. It only remained to be seen how he intended to do it.

Would he murder her himself or would other of his hired assailants throw her into the sea from the boat Joe had mentioned? Was that what he intended to do, she wondered, or had he other plans? Would he, perhaps, stab her to death and then throw her body overboard? She wanted to shriek out loud as a sudden panic swept over her.

She did not want to die. She wanted to live, and it was with the utmost difficulty she stopped herself from struggling helplessly against the blanket that covered her, making a wild, hopeless effort to throw herself from the coach. It would be quite fruitless, she knew that. It was more than likely that Joe would knock her senseless if she attempted it.

She had felt hot and suffocated before, but now she felt bitterly cold, the chill of fear creeping over her. She was helpless and alone. There was only the darkness, these two frightening men and the clomp, clomp of the horses' hooves carrying her to some unknown and terrifying destination.

She felt the tears of helplessness gather in her eyes. She had never felt so young, so childlike in her desolation. She wanted her mother, her father. She wanted to cry out to them to save her. Then she found herself whispering a prayer.

"Please, God, don't let them hurt me. Please, God, don't let them kill me."

She knew as she prayed that only God could save her from the predicament she was in now. On two other occasions she had come up against Lord Wroxhall, but each time the Marquis had been there. He had arrived just in the nick of time.

She had been well aware of the danger in which she stood. There was a ruthlessness and cruelty about Lord Wroxhall which could not be disguised by his oily voice or his elaborate, dandified appearance. She had known he was evil from that very first moment in Stade Hall. She had known it as she stepped out into Berkeley Square and been afraid that he would use violence to take her into his house. And if he wanted something, he would stick at nothing. He was determined to be rid of Maria. He had sworn it, and now he had put his plan into operation.

It had been a clever plan, for if, indeed, Maria had set out in the coach for the Marine Pavilion, it would have been morning before anyone had the least idea that anything was amiss. Then it would have been too late. That lovely body, that spun-gold hair, those melting hazel eyes would be lying at the bottom of the sea and there would be no-one to tell the tale of what had happened.

Gretna was praying again.

"God, help me! God, make them realise it is me before it is too late. Don't let them spring on me suddenly. Don't let them throw me in the water when I am not expecting it."

It was the unknown that was so horrible, that seemed to be gathering in on her, choking her, chilling her whole body so that she felt as if already the hand of death was upon her.

She tried to be glad that Maria was not in her place. She tried to think of what Maria would do in such circumstances. But somehow she could only see her lying asleep, deeply asleep, a faint smile on her lips as if she dreamed of the man she loved, her golden hair flowing over the pillow.

Again Gretna saw that certificate of marriage staring up at her from the box which Maria always kept beside her. She and the Prince were married and Maria had the courage to keep silent under the most intolerable insults, under the most unbearable slights. If she was brave enough for that, she would be brave enough to face the far lesser ordeal of physical hurt.

"I must think. I must plan. I must not give up. I must fight!" Gretna thought; and then a sudden longing for the Marquis swept over her.

Why wasn't he here? Why couldn't she run to him, as

she had done before, and hide her face against his broad shoulder? He was angry with her, she knew that. And yet in such circumstances as these she knew that he would save her; he would hold her closely to him; she would be safe, safe in his arms though the devil himself threatened her.

She felt herself longing for him with such intensity and with every fibre of her body that she felt as if the very urgency and desperation of her need must reach him, must tell him, wherever he was, that she was in danger.

Then she thought perhaps he was at the theatre, waiting to take the lovely Eloise out to supper, and she knew, with a new kind of despair, there was no hope for her there.

They must have been driving for nearly three-quarters of an hour and from the ugly snorts beside her she guessed that Joe had fallen asleep. But the other man was still awake. She could feel him fidgeting about, moving his hands and his feet. She imagined that he was twisting his head to see if, by the light of the candle-lamps, he could see which way they were going.

Then suddenly she felt a rough hand touch and grasp her ankle. She gave a scream and kicked violently with her other foot to dislodge the hands which, to her relief, set her free.

"Her's alive!" came a triumphant cry.

"Here, what's oop?" Joe woke from his sleep.

"Her's alive."

"Of course her be alive. We had no instructions to finish her off, did we? Likely as not he'll be a-waiting to see her. Stow yer gab whiles we be there."

The carriage was going downhill. It came suddenly to a standstill. One of the men had opened the window. Gretna felt the rush of cold air against her feet.

"There's th' boat," Joe remarked. "Bring the fancy mort along."

She wanted to struggle then, but it was too late. Rough arms picked her up as if she were a baby and carried her from the carriage across the cobbled stones of what she imagined might be a quay.

She knew then that she was to be drowned; taken out in a boat, weighted perhaps, and dropped overboard. She tried to scream, tried to cry out. But no sound came from her throat. She felt herself put down with a bump and knew that she was lying on the floor of a rowing-boat. She could feel the movement of the water, hear the oars being got out. There was a clink of money. She guessed that Joe and his timid friend were being paid off.

She made one last desperate effort to struggle, but the blanket had been wound too tightly round her shoulders and arms. She could only move her legs and was afraid that her skirts would blow up and she would be unable to pull them down again. Someone jumped into the boat.

"Cast off," he said.

A chain rattled into the stern. Now they were moving, two men rowing hard, so hard that she could hear their grunts and the deep intakes of their breath. She knew then that it was hopeless. There was nothing she could do. She was doomed.

She found herself thinking again of the Marquis. He would never know that she died loving him; and because he would never know it, she found herself whispering her love.

"I love you! I loved you, I think from that very first moment. I did not know it until you drew me to you at Stade Hall and I sat at your feet looking up at you. Something happened then, something strange and lovely which seemed to tingle right through me. I was afraid, and yet I was not afraid of what I saw in your eyes. It was what I had always longed for, dreamed about, and imagined would happen to me one day. But when it came I did not realise what it was. It was love. Oh, I love you!"

She felt the tears coursing down her cheeks with the intensity of her feelings. So concentrated was she on her thoughts of the Marquis that she did not realise that the men had stopped rowing until she felt one of them lift her shoulders, another take her feet.

She knew then that this was the moment when she would die, when she would feel the dark waters of the English Channel close over her. She tried to pray, tried to force herself to die bravely.

"God . . . God, take me!"

It was an effort to say the words, to force them to her lips. Then suddenly she was thrown not into the water but over a man's shoulder, and before she could recover from her surprise she realised that he was climbing. He was moving up a ladder; and after the first startled second she knew it was a rope-ladder up the side of a ship.

She could hear the creak of the timbers, the soft lap of the waves. Someone was giving orders in a modulated tone. Then she knew she was being carried across the deck, down several steps. She was set down, someone took the blanket from off her head, and then, before she could collect herself, before she could open her eyes, she heard a door close.

Very slowly, as if she awoke from a dark and terrifying dream, she moved her hands. She was free. Slower still, and only by an effort of will, she opened her eyes. She was seated on a couch in a ship's cabin. The ceiling was low and from it hung several lanterns illuminating the table, the chairs, the portholes covered with velvet curtains.

It was a luxurious cabin such as she had never imagined possible in a ship. There were expensive rugs on the floor, the couch on which she sat was covered with brocade, there were soft, satin cushions on either side of her.

She pushed back the hood which covered her head and rubbed her eyes to make sure she was not dreaming. Then she took several deep breaths as if to free her lungs from the stifling suffocation of the blanket that had covered her.

She was alive! She was not dead! And in the utter relief of not experiencing what she had expected, she felt almost light-headed. She had been so afraid when they lifted her up that it had seemed as if her very heart stopped beating with the fear of death.

No, she was not dead, but she was aboard a yacht. She knew by the sounds outside the cabin that they were putting to sea. She could hear the anchor being wound up; she could hear commands being given. sails being hoisted, the slap of bare feet running across the deck.

Where could she be going? she wondered, and thought for one moment of going on deck. She would reveal who she was to the sailors. She would ask them to refuse to obey orders and to carry her back. She ran towards the door and strove to lift the latch. It resisted her and frantically she pressed it upwards with both her hands, but it was to no avail. She realised then that the door was locked on the outside. She was a prisoner.

She crossed the cabin again and as she did so caught a reflection of herself in a mirror hanging on the wall. For a moment she hardly recognised the wild-eyed, tousle-haired girl who faced her. Then she stood still and after a moment began skilfully to repair the damage the blanket over her head had done to her appearance.

She must be calm and dignified, she told herself. Sooner or later someone would come to the cabin—the Captain of the ship perhaps. She would speak to him, tell him there had been a mistake and demand to be taken back to Brighthelmstone.

She smoothed her hair, wiped away the traces of tears from her eyes; and then, taking off her fur-edged cape, rearranged the laces at the neck of her gown. It was a pretty gown of pale blue silk sprigged with tiny flowers. It was a gown she often wore when she and Maria were alone because it was simple and easy to put on and because Maria had declared it was her favourite.

"If it is not the Captain I will send for him," Gretna thought. "I will speak to him very calmly. I will tell him who I am and explain there has been a mistake. He will obey me only if he is impressed by me. I must not look like a frightened child but like a woman who is incensed by the insulting behaviour of strangers."

Satisfied with her appearance, Gretna moved slowly across the cabin and sat herself down again on the couch, spreading her skirts out and linking her fingers together in a pathetic effort at looking relaxed and unafraid.

She had hardly done so when she heard the key turn in the lock, the latch was lifted. Gretna looked towards it, her chin held high, her eyes steady; and then, when she saw who had entered, she felt all her pretences drop away from her and the words she would have spoken die constricted in her throat.

For it was Lord Wroxhall who came into the cabin, wearing a dark cloak, his thick, sensuous lips smiling as if with pleasure at the thought of who was waiting for him.

If Gretna was surprised and dismayed to see him, it was nothing to his utter astonishment at seeing her. For a moment he stopped dead in his tracks and could only stare at her ludicrously, the smile gone from his lips, his eyes protuding in their surprise.

"Miss Gretna!" he managed to ejaculate at length. "What in the name of Heaven brings you here?"

His surprise gave Gretna time to collect herself. She had not expected Lord Wroxhall to be here in person even though she knew it had been at his instigation that she had been kidnapped.

"I was about to ask you the same question, my Lord. How dare you have me conveyed here in such a manner?"

"But . . . you . . . you have no business on this yacht," Lord Wroxhall spluttered. "Did they bring you as well?"

"Not as well, my Lord," Gretna answered, "but instead of Mistress Fitzherbert."

"This is nonsensical, insane," Lord Wroxhall exclaimed. "How did you come to take her place?"

"I had no choice in the matter," Gretna replied. "When those hired assassins of yours covered me with a blanket and carried me roughly to a waiting carriage, they imagined that I was Mistress Fitzherbert when I was, in fact, but going to His Royal Highness to explain that she was asleep and could not be disturbed."

"Thunder and turf!" Lord Wroxhall exploded. "One could not credit such imbecility."

"One could not credit that you, my Lord, who are supposed to be a nobleman, would dare to behave in such a manner to anyone, least of all one who is loved by His Royal Highness, the Prince of Wales."

"The whole thing is impossible! How could I imagine the sapskulls would so misunderstand my instructions?" Lord Wroxhall said, striding about the room.

"Well, as they have done so, I suggest you stop this ship and let me return immediately to Brighthelmstone," Gretna said.

Lord Wroxhall stopped still and looked at her.

"Return!" he ejaculated. "There's no return for you."

She felt herself blanch at his words, but her eyes did not flicker as she asked bravely:

"What does your Lordship mean by that?"

"I mean," he said roughly, "that you have burned your boats, my girl. You have come here in Mistress Fitzherbert's place. Well then, here you will have to stay. How can I take you back and allow you to chatter of what has happened? I have no desire to lose my standing in Society."

"Whatever standing you may have, my Lord," Gretna retorted, "I can promise you it will be safe with me. I have no desire to talk of what has happened this evening. I am merely ashamed that anyone in your position should have sunk to such depths of iniquity merely because of some monstrous wager made in a moment of inebriety."

Lord Wroxhall's eyebrows went up.

"So you know of that, do you?"

"I overheard you, my Lord, at Carlton House!"

"You overheard! Did you speak of it to anyone?"

"No, indeed," Gretna said quickly. "I would not have lowered myself to relate anything so despicable."

Even as she spoke and saw the relief on his face she realised that she had made a mistake. She saw all too late that the one thing he was afraid of was that he might be connected in any way with the crime he had been about to commit. He would have covered his tracks, had an alibi which was unshakable, in case anyone should in any way question him as to the disappearance of Maria Fitzherbert.

"So nobody knows, do they?" he said silkily, and she saw that his assurance had returned and now he was looking at her in a very different manner from what he had done previously.

"Perhaps, after all," he said softly. "I am not so much the loser as I thought. Mistress Fitzherbert has not come aboard, but Gretna is here in her stead—little Gretna who has been very unkind to me up till now."

Gretna rose to her feet.

"My Lord, let us cease this exchange of words. Command the Captain of this ship to put back to shore immediately. Take me back to Brighthelmstone and I promise you, I give you my word of honour, that I will never speak of what has occurred this night."

"And wouldn't I be a fool to trust your word?" Lord Wroxhall said. "Can you really expect me to relinquish the spoils of victory so easily? A victory which I had almost thought was lost to me when you ran away from me in Berkeley Square."

"My Lord, I command you to do as I say," Gretna said with a little quiver in her voice.

In answer Lord Wroxhall unclasped the black cloak he was wearing and she saw that beneath it he was dressed in a velvet coat with embroidered collar and that his waistcoat buttons were of sapphires and diamonds. She guessed then that he had come straight to the ship from some social function—perhaps the theatre, perhaps a dinner at which everyone afterwards would swear he was in particularly good form and could not in any way be connected with the disappearance of a certain notorious lady.

As Gretna stood watching him, he tidied his cravat and then turned towards her, a smile on his thick, sensuous lips.

"We are going on a little trip together, my dear," he said. "So let us enjoy ourselves. Tomorrow, or perhaps the next day, it will be realised that we have both disappeared. What will the gossips say, I wonder? That you succumbed eventually to my ardency."

"I will go on no trip with you, my Lord," Gretna cried.

"You have no choice in the matter," he replied softly. "You have come here unasked and uninvited, but nothing, I assure you, could give me greater pleasure. I was to have returned to Brighthelmstone tonight. Now I shall do nothing of the sort. This is my yacht; the Captain will obey my orders whatever they may be. The world is before us. Where would you wish to go? To Spain? The Mediterranean? Or even, perhaps to some golden island from which we need only return when we are tired of one another?" He stood in front of her speaking slowly and silkily, and all the time his eyes were devouring her, taking in every detail of her little frightened face and the sudden quickening movement of her breasts beneath the laces of her gown.

"You cannot ... mean that, my Lord," Gretna stammered. "You know full well I hate and detest you. I have given you my word that I will not betray your perfidy. Tease me no longer, but ... let us return."

"I am not teasing you," he answered. "I am telling you what we are about to do. A honeymoon, little Gretna! A honeymoon such as you have never dreamed possible. But we have no need of a parson, you and I. The legal ties will be but an encumbrance when love no longer interests us and we wish to be rid of each other."

"I would not ... marry you if you went down on your knees to ask me," Gretna stormed.

"And as I have no intention of marrying you," he jeered, "such fire is quite unnecessary. But as I have told you before, it delights me to see you in a rage. When your eyes are flashing you are infinitely more beautiful than at any other time."

He had not touched her, but his assurance and the way he was looking at her made Gretna feel as if his big hands and thick lips besmirched her. She gave a little cry of horror and turned from him, looking wildly round the cabin.

"I cannot ... escape you, my Lord," she said desperately. "I know that. So I must ask you, if you have a spark of decency within you, to take me back. I ... beg you to do so; to be ... merciful."

He laughed.

"So now you are pleading with me," he said. "This is,

indeed, a different tone. You will plead with me a great deal more, little Gretna, before I have finished with you. The first time we met I told you that you were a filly that was unbroken. Well, it will amuse me to break you, to hear you plead with me, to watch you cry out because you are afraid. Nothing is more boring than a woman who loves too easily. I think I shall enjoy our . . . honeymoon."

"You cannot mean it, you . . . cannot!" Gretna cried. "I beg of you, my Lord, to listen to me. You cannot do this thing. You know that it is wrong, wicked . . . evil, because I am only a woman, I have no strength to fight you . . . physically. Spare me . . . and I will be grateful to you for the rest of my life."

"While I should never forgive myself for relinquishing what I had won before I had even tasted the delights of conquest," he answered.

"Please! Please!" Gretna begged, clasping her hands together, the tears starting to her eyes.

He chuckled thickly in his throat.

"Delightful," he said. "Delightful. And how pretty you look in your anxiety! We have plenty of time for such theatricals. Let us drink some wine together. Beautiful women and wine go well together."

There was a bell lying on the table. He picked it up and rang it. Almost immediately a servant appeared at the door.

"Bring me a decanter of wine," Lord Wroxhall commanded.

And then, as the man made to turn, Gretna moved forward.

"Wait!" she said. "I . . ."

She got no further. Somehow she could not bring herself to make a scene in front of a servant; and as if he sensed her dilemma, Lord Wroxhall laughed again and said:

"The lady is but asking that you should bring champagne, and make haste about it."

The man went from the cabin. Gretna covered her face with her hands and sank down on a chair. Lord Wroxhall watched her bowed head with a smile of satisfaction and, picking up his quizzing-glass, twirled it by the ribbon with which it was attached to his neck.

"Such despair is quite unnecessary, my dear Gretna," he said at length. "We shall deal well together, I am quite convinced of that. You must have seen enough of the *beau monde* by this time to realise that young women of your sort are best provided with a protector. And I, if I may say so, am not only a very experienced, but undoubtedly a generous one."

"How dare you speak to me like that!" Gretna replied, raising her head, her voice vibrant with anger. "I am not a woman of that sort and you know it full well. My mother may have eloped with my father, but my grandfather was a nobleman and my father came of gentle stock."

"And you, my dear," Lord Wroxhall retorted, "are the guest of the most notorious woman of 'that sort' in the whole length and breadth of the British Isles—Mistress Fitzherbert, mistress of His Royal Highness The Prince of Wales."

Gretna bit her lip. With the utmost difficulty she prevented herself from throwing the truth in his face; from telling him that Maria was married in the sight of God and in sight of man. What would he say if he knew that she was the legal wife of the Heir Apparent to the Throne, a wife who kept her marriage certificate a secret because it would harm the husband she loved too well?

"You see, you have nothing to say," Lord Wroxhall sneered. "And so your scruples are unnecessary and as useless as your pleas for mercy. Let us enjoy ourselves. Ah! Here is the wine."

The servant came into the cabin carrying a silver tray on which there was the champagne, a decanter of red wine and crystal glasses.

"Set it down," Lord Wroxhall commanded. "I will help myself."

"Very good, m'Lord. The Captain asked me to convey his compliments and to say that a Revenue cutter was signalling as to the name of the ship and your Lordship's destination."

"Tell them to go to hell," Lord Wroxhall snapped. "These Revenue cutters are a menace."

"Yes, m'Lord," the man answered impassively.

"No, on second thoughts," Lord Wroxhall said as he reached the door, "tell the Captain to signal that our destination is France. It is what they will expect."

"Very good, m'Lord."

The man went from the cabin. Lord Wroxhall poured out a glass of champagne and carried it across the cabin to Gretna.

"Drink this, my dear," he said. "Perhaps it will warm

your heart a little towards someone who is, I asssure you, entranced by your beauty."

In answer Gretna rose to her feet and struck the glass from his hand. It fell to the floor and smashed into a thousand pieces.

"Enough of this farce," she said. "I have told you that I will not stay with you, and I mean it. Turn back or put me ashore in France. If you do not, I swear that I will fling myself overboard."

He looked at her for a moment, laughing gently, and then he reached out and took her in his arms. She struggled against him, fighting with all her strength, to no avail.

Slowly, inexorably, he pulled her close to him, drawing her closer, closer, until, although she twisted and turned her head desperately, his fingers turned her face up to his. She felt a shudder of revulsion and horror pass through her as his hot, greedy mouth captured hers and held it captive.

She felt once again as if she was being suffocated, as she had felt when the blanket was thrown over her head. His kiss nauseated her and yet she could not be free of him. He was too strong. He held her crushed to him, kissing her until she felt she must swoon away from the very horror of it.

He drew her nearer still, held her with one arm as if in a vice, his free hand caressing her neck and her bare shoulders, pulling at the laces at her breast, until she cried out, struggling frantically against him. Then as she heard her gown tear she freed herself from him by an almost frenzied effort.

She ran from him to the other side of the cabin. She got behind the couch and pushed it forward so that it stood between them. She stood there, her breath coming sobbingly from between her lips.

"So unspoilt, so inexperienced!" he said softly. "What a pleasure to teach you what love means!"

"How can you . . . defame the word?" she panted. "This is not . . . love. This is . . . lust. This is all that I have ever heard of . . . beastliness . . . horror and . . . de-defilement."

She was crying as she spoke, both with anger and fear. Then she realised suddenly that her defiance was exciting him. She knew it by the glint in his eyes, the smile on his lips, the way his fingers moved a little as if he was holding her and touching her again.

"Let me go! Let me go!" she pleaded in a sudden terror. "You cannot . . . do this to me! You cannot!"

"So small, so helpless, so very ineffectual," he said in his silky voice. And he started across the cabin towards her.

She knew then that he was stalking her, stalking her as he had tried to do that first night at Stade Hall. The huntsman after his prey, a-thrill with the chase, conscious all the time that for the fleeing animal there was no escape.

She stood trembling behind the couch, holding on to the back of it and then moving a little, first to the right and then to the left, as he advanced.

"I shall catch you eventually," he jeered, and unexpectedly he reached over towards her.

She gave a scream, tried to run. It was too late! His long arms had hold of her and now they prevented her from escaping. He was moving round the couch and had her once again in his embrace.

She struggled again, fighting against him, beating at him with her hands and realising as she did so how weak and ineffectual she was. His eyes were afire with passion, his lips were wet with desire, his evil lust gave him an almost super-human strength. She was helpless and he did not even feel the blows she aimed at him for his hands were on her, tearing at her gown.

And now, once again, his mouth had taken possession of hers and he was forcing her down on to the couch. It was then, as she felt herself drowning with the full terror of what he would do to her, as her heart thumped unevenly, as the desperateness of her plight seemed to make her limbs turn to water, she heard the cabin door open.

Lord Wroxhall's mouth freed hers and she gasped for breath. She heard him mutter an oath of annoyance. She turned to escape from him, putting her hands up to her torn dress with an instinctive modesty even while, in the desperateness of her plight, she cared for nothing save for the moment's respite.

And then she saw who stood there, his broad shoulders seeming to fill the doorway, his head almost against the ceiling. There was an anger on his face such as she had never seen before, an anger which seemed to transform him for a moment from a man into an avenging angel.

"You!" gasped Lord Wroxhall.

"Yes, I," replied the Marquis.

He walked across the room very slowly and then, before Lord Wroxhall could say any more, before he could hardly move from where he was standing at the side of the couch, the Marquis hit him. He hit him hard in the face with first one hand and then the other.

Lord Wroxhall staggered and fell to the floor.

"How dare you touch me!" he snarled. "If you want me to give you satisfaction I will do so."

"Get up!" the Marquis commanded. "I will take my satisfaction here and now."

Lord Wroxhall got to his feet and made for the door.

"Sailors! Captain! Help . . ." he yelled.

But his words were cut off in midstream. The Marquis hit him again and yet again, the blood streaming from his nose, one eye seeming to close up. And then as he tried to stagger to his feet, he went down from another blow on the chin.

The Marquis stood over him and his face was no longer that of an avenging angel, but that of a devil twisted into an anger and a fury that made him almost unrecognisable.

"Get up, you unspeakable swine! I've not finished with you yet," he said between his teeth, and there was murder in his eyes.

It was then that Gretna put her hand on his arm.

"Do not kill him," she pleaded.

The Marquis looked down at her. It appeared to her that the expression on his face did not change.

"Do not kill him," Gretna said again. "Take me . . . away. Please take me . . . away."

In answer the Marquis bent down and picked up Lord Wroxhall by the lapels of his velvet coat. He was a pitiable sight. The Marquis held him for a moment, looking at his abject, snivelling, bloody face with satisfaction. Then he said:

"Listen to me, Wroxhall. Go away and do not dare come back. If you do, I swear that everyone shall hear of what has happened this night. Set one foot on English soil and the whole world shall know what you tried to do and how you failed. You will not only be exiled, but you will be the laughing-stock of the Society you value so highly. Now, go to hell, and quickly!"

He flung him contemptuously on the floor.

"Get your cloak," he said curtly to Gretna.

"It is . . . here," she faltered, taking it from the chair on which she had laid it.

She put it round her and he made no effort to help her.

His face was stern and uncompromising. She pulled the hood up over her head. As he held open the door for her to pass through it, she looked up at him for a moment with an appeal in her eyes. She wanted to thank him, but no words would come to her lips.

"The Revenue cutter is alongside," he said coldly, and she knew by the look on his face there was no forgiveness for her there.

12

THE MARQUIS OF Stade sat down to breakfast with the air of a man who has been asked to eat at his own funeral. He declined the appetising dishes that his man brought him one by one, and finally contented himself with merely picking at a lamb cutlet.

"What is the time, Masters?" he asked in the tone of one who would not be surprised if he was told it was the crack of doom.

" 'Tis five minutes past noon, m'Lord," Masters said in a respectful tone, and added: "What does your Lordship wish me to do with the money you brought home last night?"

The Marquis glanced briefly at the pile of gold coins and notes which stood on a side-table where he had laid them after he returned from the gaming-rooms. He did not answer and Masters went on:

"There is also the money that you won the night before and the night before that, m'Lord. 'Tis not wise, if you will forgive my saying so, to have so much of value in this house. There are not the same precautions or a strong room in which to place it such as we have at Stade Hall."

The Marquis pushed his plate away with a sudden clatter.

"Give it away," he said abruptly.

"Give it away, m'Lord!" Masters ejaculated, startled for the moment out of his usual correct impassivity.

"Yes, give it away. Take it to the nearest parson and tell him to distribute it amongst the poor—there are enough of them in Brighthelmstone."

"But, m'lord, there are thousands——"

"Do as I say."

"Very good, m'Lord."

Masters withdrew from the room only to return a few seconds later.

"Mistress Fitzherbert wishes a word with you, m'Lord."

"Who?"

The Marquis rose to his feet, looking towards his man as if he could not have heard him aright.

"Mistress Fitzherbert, m'Lord."

She had come into the room as Masters spoke, looking extraordinarily bewitching in a hat trimmed with plumes that matched her simple gown of soft grey satin. There was a light scarf over her shoulders. She pulled it around her a little nervously as if the Marquis's frowning countenance made her a little uneasy, and then she smiled at him disarmingly.

"I apologise, my Lord, for intruding upon you."

" 'Tis no intrusion, Madam, but an unexpected honour," the Marquis said stiffly; then remembering his manners, he added: "Will you not be seated, Madam?"

Maria crossed the room, her gown rustling softly as she moved, and seated herself in an armchair which faced the sunlight streaming through the long windows which overlooked the Marine Parade.

The Marquis followed slowly to stand opposite her on the hearthrug, his back to the empty fireplace, his eyes fixed on her as if he could scarcely credit her presence in his sitting-room.

"Had I known you were calling on me," he said at length, as if he felt some apology was necessary, "I would have received you in the Salon upstairs. This is but the breakfast-room. I was late last night."

It was unusual for him to explain his actions, and as if she understood that he was speaking to fill in the time until they came down to business, she said quietly:

"You are surprised to see me, my Lord. I have come because I need your help."

The Marquis raised his eyebrows.

"My help, Madam!"

"Yes. Gretna has disappeared."

If she had expected to surprise him, she succeeded. He was suddenly rigid, his eyes staring at her almost ferociously.

"It is impossible!" he exclaimed. "Quite impossible!"

"Perhaps I should explain," Maria said. "She has gone of her own free will. She left a note behind for me. But I am worried—very worried, and that is why I have come to ask for your assistance."

"Why has she gone?" the Marquis asked.

"That is perhaps something you can explain to me," Maria replied. "You see, she has been unwell these past three days."

"I had no idea," the Marquis said.

"She seemed feverish and exhausted three days ago—on Wednesday morning to be exact. I remember because I, myself, was ill on Tuesday night and went to bed early. I sent for my physician—he also attends His Royal Highness—but he found nothing very wrong with her save a fever and what he described as an unusual exhaustion."

Maria gave a little sigh.

"I hoped she would recover quickly and, indeed, yesterday morning she seemed quite her own self."

She paused and looked down a moment as if she was trying to find the right words in which to go on. And then, as the Marquis said nothing, she continued:

"A friend—or rather, shall we say an acquaintance—called on me yesterday. She told me that she thought I ought to know what was the latest *on dit* of Brighthelmstone. It was, my Lord, that on Tuesday night, the evening on which I had retired to bed early, Gretna ran away with Lord Wroxhall and was brought back by you, my Lord, in the early hours of the morning."

Maria's soft voice finished speaking. The Marquis made no answer although she looked up at him enquiringly. He was frowning, his dark eyebrows almost meeting across the bridge of his aristocratic nose and his mouth was set in a hard line.

"How could this have got about?" he asked.

"I think perhaps you owe me an explanation, my Lord," Maria said.

"Did you speak to Gretna of this?" he enquired.

"Indeed I did," Maria replied. "She did not deny it, but it was obvious that she was not being frank with me. I begged her to tell me the truth, but she excused herself by saying it was not her secret. All she affirmed, over and over again, was that she had not tried to elope with Lord Wroxhall. But she would not deny that she had returned with you to my house in the early hours or that in some way that I could not fathom you had rescued her—from whom I do not understand."

Maria twisted her hands together and added passionately:

"I wish I had said nothing to her. I wish, indeed, I had not plagued her. But later in the afternoon she complained of a headache and retired to her bedchamber. This morning, when the maid went to call her, there was only this note on her pillow."

She fumbled in her reticule and brought out a note which she held out to the Marquis. He took it from her and, still scowling, read it through slowly:

My dearest Maria,

I have thought Things over very Carefully and I have gone Away. If I Stay, I shall only bring Disgrace and Scandal on You and that I cannot Bear to do, for I love You so Dearly. Also, I am costing You Monies which you can Ill Afford. You have been so Generous, so Kind to me and for that I thank You from my whole Heart.

I shall be in Safe Keeping, so You must not Worry about me, and I shall find Suitable Employment so that I can earn my own Living and be a Burden to no-one.

Pray do not try to find me, it will only be an Embarrassment to You. I Love You and I Thank You.

Gretna.

"Can you imagine what I felt when I received that letter?" Maria asked with a little break in her voice. "How can Gretna find employment or, indeed, how can she look after herself? When she speaks of costing me monies, that fear of hers was entirely my fault."

"Why?" the Marquis asked, his voice expressionless and yet somehow Maria felt he was not unsympathetic.

"Yesterday, after luncheon, the Prince wished to go to the races and we found that we were so short of money we could not raise even five pounds between us. We laughed about it, and then my old maid, who has been with me for nearly twenty years, begged us to accept her savings so as to tide us over our difficulties.

"We refused her, of course, but both the Prince and I were deeply touched at her offer. I think that Gretna must have been disturbed that she herself had no money."

Maria gave a little sob.

"I blame myself utterly for not thinking then that such

a scene must be an embarrassment to her. But I have been so happy to have her with me, I love her so dearly that I could not suspicion even for a moment she might be thinking of leaving."

"Have you no idea where she has gone?" the Marquis enquired.

"None at all," Maria replied. "I have been cudgelling my brains all the morning as to where she was likely to go or where, indeed, she could have hoped to find employment."

"Could she have gone back to London?"

"Pray Heaven she has not! If she has, you must find her, my Lord, for I cannot bear to think of her alone and defenceless in that great heartless city. But what puzzles me is why she should think it necessary to run away. What scandal could be attached to her name? Will you not tell me what occurred on Tuesday night?"

There was a pause and then the Marquis said:

"You have no idea what happened?"

"None at all, I swear it," Maria replied in a bewildered tone.

"What Gretna did not tell you," the Marquis said, "was that Lord Wroxhall had made a diabolical plot to kidnap you, Madam, and transport you to the West Indies."

"Me! To transport me!" Maria exclaimed. "But why? For what reason?"

"I think you can guess the reason," the Marquis said.

Maria went very pale.

"I had no idea he was my enemy," she said, her hand going suddenly to her throat.

"He did not intend you to think so," the Marquis said harshly. "It was a clever plot and might well have succeeded. You were to be taken aboard his yacht, while he, except for an hour or so during the evening, had a perfect alibi. The yacht would have sailed away without anyone knowing where it was going, and weeks later, after the hue and cry of your disappearance had perhaps begun to die down, the Prince would have received a letter from you saying that you could stand poverty and the discomforts of your life with him no longer and so you had gone abroad. It would have been written in your own hand, Madam, because you would have been forced to write it."

"I . . . I cannot believe it," Maria said faintly. "And Gretna? How did Gretna know of this?"

"She did not," the Marquis said grimly. "They thought

to kidnap you by luring you from your house with a false message from the Prince that he desired your presence immediately. But you were asleep and Gretna could not waken you and so she went in your stead."

"It was the night I had taken laudanum!" Maria exclaimed. "No, indeed, she would not have been able to waken me."

"It was not until she was actually on board," the Marquis continued, "that Lord Wroxhall discovered what a mistake had been made. He then decided not to return to Brighthelmstone, as he had intended, but to go on a cruise with Gretna. He has always lusted after her since the first moment he saw her."

"Poor child, how frightened she must have been!" Maria breathed. "And you . . . you, my Lord, saved her?"

"Yes, by the Grace of God," the Marquis replied. "Harry Carrington discovered that some plot was afoot from a friend of Lord Wroxhall's called Sir Joseph Tanfield. He was in his company and drank most indiscreetly in the gaming-room to "the end of Mistress Fitzherbert". Harry thought it a strange toast and pressed him further, plying him with drink until he talked quite freely.

"It was then, when Harry realised what was happening, that he came in search of me. I was not far behind the assailants who had been sent to kidnap you, for I arrived at your house only twenty minutes after they had left. I asked for you and was told by a rather surprised maidservant that you were in bed."

"I insisted on her going upstairs to make sure there was no mistake. I was just about to leave, thinking that Harry had been misinformed, when something prompted me to ask for Gretna."

"It must have been the child's guardian angel who suggested it to you!" Maria cried.

"Perhaps it was," the Marquis agreed. "The maid went to search for her and when she had gone, a poor woman sitting in the hall volunteered the information that she had gone to the Marine Pavilion. She told me what had passed. A servant in the Royal livery had brought a message that the Prince desired to see you immediately. Gretna had gone in your place.

"I wasted no more time. I remembered noticing the day before that a yacht was lying in the mouth of the river some ten miles from here. My greys covered the distance in record time; but, when I arrived, the yacht had weighed anchor and was just putting out to sea."

"Dear God, what did you do?" Maria breathed.

She was listening to him fascinated, bending forward in her chair, her hands clasped tightly together as if she could hardly bear the suspense.

"I saw a Revenue cutter moving down the river. I explained to the officer who I was and told him it was imperative that I should board the yacht immediately. He was, I am glad to say, extremely obliging."

The Marquis ceased speaking and Maria said quickly:

"Is that all? What happened when you got aboard?"

"I arrived in time," the Marquis said drily. "Gretna had been badly frightened by his Lordship, but I made sure that he will not trouble either her or you again—in fact, he will not return to England."

"You did not kill him?" Maria asked.

The Marquis shook his head.

"No, Gretna was frightened of that, but I made his punishment more severe. He is one of those parasites who cannot live without the *beau monde* on which to feed his vanity."

"And Gretna, what did she say?"

"She said very little."

"She must have been overjoyed to see you."

"She would have been glad to see anyone, I think, in the circumstances," the Marquis said drily.

Maria took a deep breath.

"I came to you this morning, my Lord, not only because you are a kinsman of Gretna's, but also because I know that she has a deep tenderness for you. I hoped that perhaps you could find it in your heart to reciprocate her affection a little."

"You are mistaken, Madam," the Marquis said in his most uncompromising voice. "Gretna has told me exactly what her feelings are where I am concerned. I have no illusions about them."

"And when she told you what her feelings were," Maria said softly, "was it not on the occasion when you came to my house in St. James's Square and asked her to leave me?"

"Yes," the Marquis said briefly.

"And you believed her? Oh, what fools men are!" Maria exclaimed. "You believed that she did not care for you just because she would not obey your command to leave me—someone she had known and loved ever since she was a baby?"

She paused for a moment and then she said:

"Would you, indeed, have respected her if her loyalty had been so shallow—such a superficial thing?"

The Marquis looked at her in almost a startled manner.

"I had not thought of it like that," he said.

"But of course not," Maria said scornfully. "You told her what she was to do, ordered her to desert the one friend she has ever had in all her quiet, lonely life, the one person who had known her father and mother and had proved her affection through the long years of her growing up. You ordered her peremptorily to abandon this person and expected her to obey you."

"I was only doing what I thought was best for her," the Marquis said.

"Of course," Maria agreed. "But you could hardly expect her to think of herself and not of me. She believed that I needed her. I had told her so, for, indeed, she meant a great deal to me in my life. I, too, am lonely at times."

She saw the Marquis was frowning over her words and went on:

"Gretna has never confided in me where you are concerned, my Lord; but perhaps because I love her so deeply I am extra sensitive and perhaps a little intuitive where she is concerned. I have known that Gretna has loved you since the first moment she arrived in London."

"It is not true," the Marquis said harshly.

He walked towards the window and stood with his back to Maria, staring out at the glistening sea, but she had the idea that he was looking into the darkness of his soul and his eyes were blind to the sunlight.

"I only tell you this, my Lord, because there is no-one else to whom I can turn in my anxiety, in my fear for Gretna." She went on: "I would not have the fact that she has disappeared talked about. You know what gossips will make of such a story. And I had hoped—though, indeed, without much assurance—that you, too, might be worried about her."

The Marquis turned round at that.

"I will find her," he said. "You can rest assured that I will find her."

Maria rose to her feet.

"Thank you," she said with deep sincerity. "Thank you more than I can say. And I know the Prince will be grateful to you. He is deeply fond of Gretna, and he is fond of you, too, my Lord."

"It is gracious of you to tell me that," the Marquis said with a note of humility in his voice. "You know that I have been your enemy and yet you are generous enough to say such things to me."

"I have known that you do not like me," Maria replied. "But the Prince values your friendship, and I know that you are a good influence on him; not like some who claim the same position. That is much more important to me than anything that concerns myself."

She faltered over the last words. The Marquis stared at her with a strange expression on his face, and then he said suddenly:

"Dare I ask you to forgivè me, Madam? I was utterly wrong in all I thought and in all I imagined about you. May I humbly beg your pardon and ask you when you think of me again to think of me not as an enemy but as someone who not only wishes you well but is always at your service?"

Maria's smile lit up her face.

"I have nothing to forgive, my Lord," she said. "I can understand and respect your feelings. Both the Prince and I are greatly in need of friends whom we can trust."

She held out her hand as she spoke and the Marquis raised it to his lips.

"I swear I shall not fail you," he said quietly.

For a moment Maria's fingers tightened on his.

"And you will find Gretna?" she asked.

"I will find her and bring her back to you," the Marquis vowed.

Mrs. Merryweather took two freshly baked brown loaves from the oven and set them down on the long wooden table which stretched nearly the whole length of the kitchen. Then she fetched a pat of freshly churned butter from the marble slab in the dairy and set a large, home-cured ham down on the table beside it.

She glanced at the grandfather clock in the corner of the kitchen, saw that it was getting on for five in the afternoon, and called to her youngest son, a boy of some nine summers who was plucking a chicken outside the door:

"Colin! Are you there? Run down to the cellar and bring up the ale. The men will be back from the fields in a few minutes with their bellies a-rattling for their tea."

"Aye, Mum, I'll go in a minute," was Colin's answer; and then, just as Mrs. Merryweather was about to admonish him for not obeying her more quickly, there was a clatter of horses' hooves in the yard. Looking through the window, she had a sudden glimpse of a spanking pair of greys pulling a black-and-yellow curricle and she saw young Colin run excitedly to the horses' heads as the driver stepped down into the yard.

She waited for him to come through the open door, with her hands on her hips and her jolly, fat face unsmiling and unusually severe.

"Good afternoon, Mrs. Merryweather!"

She looked up at the Marquis, her brown eyes taking in the big, calm elegance of his appearance. Then she said with an undisguised hostility:

"There's no place for you here, m'Lord, and you can take yourself and those horseflesh of yourn out of my yard as quickly as you came in."

There was a faint smile on the Marquis's lips as he advanced further into the kitchen and put his grey driving-gloves down on the edge of the table.

"You were expecting me?" he asked quietly.

"Indeed I was not," Mrs. Merryweather snorted. "And nor was that poor lamb——"

She stopped suddenly for she had seen the look of triumph in the Marquis's eyes.

"So Gretna is here then?" he said. "I thought she'd be."

"I'll not have you troubling her or making her more miserable than she is already," Mrs. Merryweather stormed. "Coming back here, looking like a wee bird that's been left out in the storm. Not a patch of colour in her cheeks and her eyes that miserable I could cry at the sight of her . . ."

She stopped for an instant, then said accusingly:

"What have you done to her—you and your smart friends? She was happy enough before she left here."

"She has been growing up, Mrs. Merryweather," the Marquis said. "You could not keep her a baby for ever."

"Growing up, indeed! With her crying on my shoulder and asking me if she could stay here until she found work.

Work! I ask you! What can she do to earn a decent living?"

"That is just what I have come to talk to her about," the Marquis said.

"And what might you be suggesting?" Mrs. Merryweather asked truculently.

The Marquis told her.

Gretna knelt on the grass in the churchyard and laid the bunch of roses she carried on the newly marked grave. There was only a plain, cheap cross. But both her father's and her mother's names were inscribed on it and beneath them were the words: *In death they were not divided*

She arranged the flowers, then from her bent head a tear dropped on to one pink petal and lay there glistening like a dewdrop.

"You are . . . together," she whispered softly. "But I am . . . alone, so terribly . . . alone. I do not know where to . . . go or what to . . . do. Can you not help . . . me? Can you not somehow tell me . . . what I must . . . do?"

It seemed there was no answer and another dewdrop glistened on another rose; and then another and another.

She was suddenly conscious that there were footsteps approaching down the path which led from the village. She bent her head still lower, hoping that whoever it was would pass by and not speak to her. But the footsteps drew nearer and then stopped.

She willed that whoever it was would go away, seeing that she was preoccupied. But after a moment or two, when nothing happened, curiosity made her turn her head and she saw who stood there.

She sprang up then with a sudden nervous movement as if she were a fawn frightened by the hunt. She stared at the Marquis and her hands went out nervously to smooth the fullness of her muslin skirts.

She was wearing the same white muslin gown, with its blue sash, that she had worn at Stade Hall the first time she had met him. But her eyes were dark with pain and unhappiness.

"Why have . . . you . . . come here?" she asked at length, seeing that he did not speak.

"I have come to take you back to Brighthelmstone," he said. "Did you really think you could go away and no-one would worry about you?"

"But I cannot go . . . back," she said quickly. "You do not . . . understand."

"I think I do," he answered. "Come, let us sit down and talk about it."

She was too weak to resist and she let him lead her to where just outside the church there was a wooden seat set between two yew trees. From there they could look over the ancient graves to where the wild rose-bushes rioted in pink-and-white profusion over the church wall and beyond to where the green meadows sloped down to a slowly moving river.

Gretna sat down on the seat and as the Marquis settled himself beside her she moved as far away from him as she could.

"I cannot go . . . back," she said in a strangled voice.

"Why not?" he enquired.

"Because someone has . . . found out," she said. "Someone has . . . talked. I cannot bring scandal and trouble upon . . . Maria. She bears enough . . . as it is."

"There will be no scandal or trouble," the Marquis said soothingly. "I will deal with whoever is spreading these lies"

"Even you cannot save me from . . . gossip," she said. "It is too intangible, too insidious. I have seen what it can . . . do and there is no . . . remedy for . . . it."

"Except, apparently, to run away?" he said drily.

"There were other . . . reasons as well," Gretna said.

"Will you tell me what they are?" he asked.

"I must earn my own . . . living," she said firmly. "I cannot batten on Maria . . . for ever. She . . . she cannot . . . afford it."

"And how do you propose to set about this formidable task?" he asked.

She hesitated at this, twisting one end of her sash between her fingers.

"I . . . I thought perhaps . . . when I had rested a little," she said hesitantly, "I would go to London—unless I was fortunate enough to find . . . something to do here."

She coloured a little and added,

"You told me once to go back to the country but I do not think I could . . . make some honest farmer . . . happy, even if there was one who . . . who wanted to marry me."

"I have a better suggestion to make," the Marquis said.

"What is it?" she enquired.

"That you should come to Stade Hall. I have a position for you there."

The blood flared suddenly in her cheeks.

"You . . . suggested . . . that once . . . before," she said.

"No, no," he said quickly. "I do not mean that! I am asking you to come as my wife."

For a moment she was very still and then she said, looking away from him:

"It is, indeed, kind and . . . generous of your Lordship to offer me . . . marriage. I well understand that you feel . . . you are obliged t . . . to do so because of what has . . . occurred and because . . . people are gossiping. I would not impose on your . . . generosity to such an . . . extent. I shall manage by . . . myself, I promise . . . you."

"And suppose I tell you that I am not being kind or generous," the Marquis said. "That I want you to come to Stade Hall."

He saw the sudden quiver of her lips, the trembling of her fingers, and then she said a little unsteadily:

"If you . . . want me, that is a different thing. But, please, there is no need to . . . marry me."

He would have spoken impetuously, but she checked him.

"Let me say it," she whispered. "When you suggested before that you should be my . . . protector, I was so stupid and ignorant that I did not understand . . . wh . . . what you meant. And now I do . . . understand, and if you would protect me from all the . . . things that . . . frighten me, then I would like, above all things, to come to you. For I think, my Lord, I should always feel . . . safe and . . . unafraid with . . . you."

Her voice died away and then she gave a little gasp. The Marquis had put out his hand and taking her chin between his fingers had turned her face towards his.

"Look at me, Gretna," he said. "Look into my eyes and listen to what I have to say. I knew that night at Stade Hall that I loved you. I knew it but, like you, I was stupid and ignorant and I did not understand. What I offered you then was an insult—not only an insult to you, my darling, but an insult to the love that we feel for each other, which has been there in our hearts since that very first moment. I knew it that night when I looked into your eyes, and we both knew it when we were joined together for one ecstatic moment on the balcony at Carlton House. Why do we waste time in fighting each other?"

She shut her eyes for a moment as if she could not bear to look at him, to feel herself tingling with excitement, to feel herself thrilling because of what he was saying. And then she opened them again and the world was even more glorious than it had been a moment before.

"Do you really think," the Marquis asked, "that I should want you in any other way save as my wife? I want to own you, to possess you, to know that you are mine and no other man may touch you or look at you because you belong to me."

He released her chin, put his arms round her and drew her close, looking down at her with a tenderness in his face which no-one had ever seen before.

"I want you to be my wife, Gretna," he said.

"But . . . I thought . . ." she murmured, "that you . . . loved Eloise."

"Who is she?" he asked. "Are there any other women in the world besides you? If there are, I have not noticed them since we first met."

She gave a little sigh of utter contentment, the breath coming quickly between her parted lips, her eyes like stars of shining glory.

"I am almost afraid to kiss you," the Marquis said, "in case you are not real, in case you will disappear again as you have disappeared so often. I am going to chain you to me from the moment we are married until the moment we die. I am so vastly afraid of losing you."

"And I thought I had lost . . . you," Gretna murmured.

"How could you have been so foolish?" he asked. "And why were you crying when I found you just now?"

She glanced for a moment towards the grave where her father and mother lay united, and then she looked up at him again and he was almost blinded by the radiance on her face.

"I was lonely," she said simply. "And now I shall never be . . . lonely again."

"Never, my darling," he assured her. "Never while we both live. I love you, Gretna. Tell me you love me."

"I . . . love . . . you with my . . . whole heart," Gretna tried to say, but the words were lost, crushed against her mouth by his lips, forgotten as the wonder and glory of his kiss made her thrill as she had never thrilled before, with an ecstasy which seemed to carry them towards the stars.

She was no longer alone. She was close in his arms. She was his.